OLIVES AND OBSESSIONS

A TUSCAN COZY MYSTERY

SOPHIE BROOKS MYSTERIES
BOOK 2

DAISY LANDISH

First Edition

Editing by Veronica Jauregui
Cover by Daisy Landish

BEACHES AND TRAILS
PUBLISHING

PREVIOUSLY ON FARM-TO-TABLE ADVENTURES

From Sophie's Substack: Farm-to-Table Adventures

Hello, dear readers! Before I share my latest adventure in Tuscany, I thought some of you might appreciate a recap of how I ended up investigating murder alongside olive oil production. If you've been following my journey from the beginning, feel free to skip ahead. For newcomers about to join me in Italy—welcome to the chaos.

The Oregon Disaster (or: How I Learned My Husband Was a Liar)

Six months ago, I, Sophie Brooks, co-owner of a successful farm-to-table restaurant in Oregon's wine country, married Ryan, and lived what I thought was my dream life. Then I discovered Ryan had been sourcing our "local, sustainable" ingredients from mass distributors while lying to our customers about our farm-to-table practices.

The betrayal wasn't just professional—it shattered everything I believed about our partnership. So I did what any rational food blogger would do: I left everything behind, sold my share of the restaurant, and started a new

Substack documenting authentic farm-to-table operations around the world.

Sonoma Healing (or: Where I Learned to Trust Myself Again)

My first stop was Sonoma, California, where I stayed at Cartwright Vineyard and slowly rebuilt my confidence while documenting their traditional winemaking methods. I also solved my first murder—because apparently, when you're running from your problems, the universe has a sense of humor about the new problems it sends your way.

The short version: vineyard owner James Cartwright was killed by developer Angela Mason, who was systematically buying up properties through fraud and intimidation. With help from local restaurant owner Nate (more on him later), I exposed her scheme, saved the vineyard, and discovered I had investigative instincts I never knew existed.

More importantly, I learned to trust my gut again. And maybe developed feelings for a certain California restaurateur who flew to Italy when I needed help, but we're getting ahead of ourselves.

Enter: Tuscany

Which brings us to Italy, where I came to document traditional olive oil production at the De Luca family's agriturismo in Montepulciano. I was invited by Marco De Luca, an 83-year-old patriarch who represented everything beautiful about preserving culinary traditions.

The Personal Stuff (Because You Keep Asking)

Yes, my divorce from Ryan is pending. Yes, Nate and I have developed something that might become something beautiful, given time and patience. No, I'm not rushing into anything—I've learned that the best transformations happen slowly, like olives pressed into golden oil.

For New Readers:

You should know that this blog started as simple food writing and has evolved into something part culinary journalism, part accidental detective work. I don't go looking for trouble—it just seems to find me in kitchens and markets around the world.

If you're here for recipes and restaurant reviews, you'll get those. If you're here for international intrigue and murder mysteries, apparently I provide those too. If you're here for personal growth and figuring out how to rebuild your life after it explodes—welcome to the club, we're all learning together.

PROLOGUE: THE SABOTEUR

The moon hung like a silver coin over the rolling hills of Montepulciano, casting long shadows between the ancient olive trees. The grove whispered in the night breeze, a thousand leaves rustling secrets that had been buried in Tuscan soil for generations. October air carried the earthy scent of approaching harvest—that rich, loamy smell of olives ready to surrender their golden treasure.

A figure moved through the darkness, footsteps muffled by centuries of fallen leaves and soft earth. They knew these paths by heart—every gnarled root that jutted from the ground like an arthritic finger, every stone boundary marker that had stood sentinel since before memory, every place where the ancient terraces dipped and rose like a sleeping giant's chest. Tonight, though, familiarity bred not comfort but a desperate, clawing urgency.

The irrigation lines snaked through the grove like silver veins, carrying life to trees that had weathered Etruscan settlements, Roman conquests, medieval plagues, and two world wars. Some of these olives had been saplings when Michelangelo walked the earth. Others were older still, their twisted trunks bearing witness to secrets that would make the living shudder.

The figure knelt beside one of the main distribution valves, hands steady despite the tremor of fear that ran through their frame like electricity. A small knife appeared from their coat pocket—nothing fancy, just a simple folding blade worn smooth by years of use. It glinted in the moonlight as it bit into the thick rubber tubing, creating not a clean cut that would suggest equipment failure, but a ragged, desperate tear that spoke of sabotage born from panic.

"*Il tempo sta finendo*," they whispered to the darkness, their voice barely audible above the olive leaves' eternal murmur. *Time is running out.*

Water began to seep from the damaged line, darkening the earth around the base of a particularly ancient tree whose trunk bore scars from centuries of careful pruning. The saboteur's breath came in short, visible puffs in the cool autumn air. This had to look natural, accidental—just another sign that the old ways were failing, that Marco De Luca's stubborn adherence to tradition was finally costing him.

But the water damage was only the beginning.

From a worn leather pouch—the kind used by farmers to carry seeds—they withdrew something far more precious than any harvest. Their fingers trembled as they unwrapped the small bundle, revealing a piece of aged parchment that seemed to glow amber in the moonlight. Even in the dim illumination, fragments of elegant Italian script were visible, written in the flowing hand of someone long dead. Property boundaries drawn in fading brown ink, official seals that time had rendered nearly illegible, and signatures that would mean everything to those who understood their significance.

The black stone boundary marker stood like a silent sentinel ten paces away, worn smooth by centuries of weather and touch. Unlike the newer concrete markers that dotted the property lines between neighboring farms, this stone was ancient—carved from local limestone and set into the earth by hands that had turned to dust generations ago. Its surface bore the faint outline of symbols: olive branches intertwined with what might have been a family crest, though time and weather had softened the details beyond easy recognition.

The figure approached the stone with reverence, as if approaching an altar. Their movements were practiced, efficient—someone who had rehearsed this moment in their mind countless times. The earth at the base of the marker gave way easily under their hands, as if it had been disturbed before. Not recently, but not so long ago that the soil had completely settled.

As they dug, memories flashed through their mind like fragments of a fever dream. A young boy playing among these very trees while his nonna told stories of old feuds and stolen land. A teenage girl discovering documents hidden in a farmhouse wall during renovations. An adult finally understanding what those documents meant—and what they could cost the people they loved most.

The wrapped parchment slipped into the shallow hole like a secret returning home. They covered it with dirt and fallen leaves, scattering a handful of olive pits over the disturbed earth to make it look undisturbed. By morning, no trace would remain of their work—just another patch of ground beneath an ancient marker that tourists photographed without understanding its significance.

A dog barked in the distance, sharp and insistent. The sound cut through the night like a knife, freezing the saboteur in place. Their heart hammered against their ribs as they tilted their head toward the sound, straining to identify its source. The bark came again, closer now, followed by the unmistakable beam of a flashlight dancing between the trees like a wayward star.

"*Merda*," they breathed, panic flaring in their chest like a struck match.

The light was moving in their direction—not random, but purposeful. Someone was coming, someone who knew the grove well enough to navigate it in darkness. The saboteur gathered their tools quickly, but not before something caught the moonlight at their throat—an antique pendant in the shape of an olive branch, its silver surface tarnished with age and worn smooth by constant handling. The pendant swayed as they moved, catching the light like a signal fire in the darkness.

Family jewelry. The kind passed down through generations, carrying with it all the weight of blood and obligation.

The flashlight beam swept closer, illuminating patches of grove in harsh white circles. Heavy footsteps crunched through the underbrush, accompanied by an elderly man's voice calling out in heavily accented Italian. "*Chi c'è là? Who's there? I know someone is in my grove!*"

Marco De Luca. Even in the darkness, even with fear singing in their veins, the saboteur recognized that voice—still strong despite his eighty-three years, still commanding despite the tremor that age had brought to his hands. The old man might be walking with a stick these days, but his hearing remained sharp as the pruning shears he wielded with such devastating precision.

The saboteur melted back into the shadows, moving with the silent grace of someone who had walked these paths since childhood. They knew exactly where to step to avoid the patches of loose stone that would shift and clatter, which routes would take them away from the approaching light without crossing open ground where the moon would expose them.

At the edge of the grove, they paused, looking back toward the damaged irrigation line where water continued to seep into the thirsty earth. In their haste, a small piece of dark fabric clung to a low olive branch—torn from their coat when they'd brushed too close in the darkness.

By morning, Marco would discover more than just the flood. The old man would find the damaged valve, run his weathered fingers over the deliberately frayed edges, and know this was no accident. But would he report it? Would he worry his family on the eve of harvest?

The pendant caught the moonlight one last time as the figure slipped through a gap in the stone wall. Behind them, Marco's voice grew louder, more agitated. "*Madonna mia!* What has happened here?"

The saboteur pulled their coat tighter and walked on, carrying their secret like a seed waiting to sprout.

CHAPTER 1
THE OLIVE GROVE WHISPERS

THE TAXI CLIMBED the winding road through the Tuscan countryside, each turn revealing another postcard-perfect vista of rolling hills dotted with cypress trees and ancient stone farmhouses. Sophie Brooks pressed her face to the window, drinking in the view that seemed painted in shades of gold and amber under the October afternoon sun. After three months in Sonoma's wine country, she thought she'd grown accustomed to breathtaking land-scapes, but Tuscany possessed a different kind of magic—older, deeper, steeped in centuries of human stories.

"*Ecco, signorina,*" the driver announced as they crested a hill. "Agriturismo De Luca."

Sophie's breath caught. The property spread before them like something from a Renaissance painting: terraced olive groves cascading down gentle slopes, a honey-colored farmhouse with terra cotta roof tiles weathered to perfection, and outbuildings that seemed to grow organi-cally from the landscape itself. Cypress trees stood like sentinels along the drive, their dark spires pointing toward a sky the color of faded denim.

But it was the olive trees that made her heart sing. Hundreds of them, their silver-green leaves shimmering in the breeze, their gnarled trunks twisted into shapes that spoke of incredible age and resilience. Some were clearly ancient, their bark scarred and weathered, while others showed the careful pruning of generations of devoted hands.

"*Bellissimo,*" she whispered, already reaching for her camera.

The taxi pulled to a stop in front of the main house, and Sophie gathered her bags with the familiar flutter of excitement that came with each new destination. This was what she'd been searching for when she left Oregon—places where food wasn't just sustenance but culture, tradition, and art combined into something that fed the soul as much as the body.

As she paid the driver, the front door of the farmhouse opened, and a woman emerged who could only be Sofia De Luca. She was perhaps forty, with the kind of natural beauty that came from a life spent in honest work—sun-kissed skin, dark hair pulled back in a practical bun, and eyes that sparkled with warmth and intelligence. She wore a simple dress in deep blue, covered by an apron that bore the evidence of recent cooking: flour dusting one side, a smear of what might have been tomato sauce near the pocket.

"Sophie!" Sofia called out, her English accented but clear. "Welcome, welcome to our home!" She hurried forward with arms outstretched, enveloping Sophie in the kind of hug that immediately made her feel like family rather than a guest.

"Sofia, thank you so much for having me," Sophie replied, breathing in the scent of herbs and wood smoke that clung to the other woman's clothes. "This place is absolutely magical."

"*Ah, bene!* You have not seen anything yet," Sofia laughed, stepping back to take Sophie's larger suitcase despite her protests. "Come, let me show you to your room, and then we will have coffee and you can meet the family. *Nonno* is very excited to meet the famous American food blogger."

They walked through the front door into a world that seemed untouched by time. The farmhouse interior was a study in rustic elegance: exposed wooden beams darkened with age, terra cotta floors worn smooth by generations of feet, and walls lined with old photographs and religious icons. The air carried the perfume of centuries—old wood, herbs drying in bundles, the lingering sweetness of bread baked in wood ovens.

"The house has been in our family for over two hundred years," Sofia explained as they climbed a narrow staircase, the wooden steps creaking pleasantly under their feet. "Each generation has added something, but we try to keep the heart the same. *Nonno* says the stones remember our stories."

Sophie's room was on the second floor, simple but charming: whitewashed walls, a bed covered in a hand-stitched quilt, and windows that looked out over the olive groves. A small writing desk sat beneath one window, already set with fresh flowers and a bowl of olives that looked like they'd been picked that morning.

"This is perfect," Sophie said, meaning it completely. After the tensions and revelations of Sonoma, this felt like exactly what her soul needed—a place where traditions ran deep and change came slowly, if at all.

"*Bene!* Settle yourself, and then come down when you are ready. We will be in the kitchen," Sofia said, pausing at the door. "And Sophie? Thank you for coming. *Nonno* has been talking about your visit for weeks. He reads your blog, you know, with my help with the English. He says you understand food the way it should be understood—not just as fuel, but as love made visible."

After Sofia left, Sophie unpacked quickly, her movements automatic after months of travel. But she found herself drawn repeatedly to the windows, mesmerized by the view. The olive groves stretched in neat rows down the hillside, their silvery leaves catching the light like water. In the distance, she could see workers moving among the trees—the harvest was in full swing, just as she'd hoped.

Her phone buzzed with a message from Oliver, and she smiled as she read it.

> Oliver: Darling, please tell me you've arrived safely and that Tuscany is everything our romantic dreams promised? I need to live vicariously through your olive oil adventures! 🫒

Sophie typed back quickly, her fingers dancing over the screen.

Sophie: Just arrived and I'm already in love. The olive groves are incredible, and Sofia (the owner's daughter) is absolutely lovely. I can already tell this is going to be special.

Oliver: Wonderful! Any handsome Italian farmers in sight? Please say yes, I need to update my fantasy life accordingly. ❚❚💚

Sophie: Too early to tell, but I'll keep you posted. Right now I'm just excited to learn about the olive oil making process. This family has been doing it for generations.

Oliver: Mmm, liquid gold. Take notes, darling—I want to know everything about how they transform those little fruits into culinary magic.

Sophie tucked her phone away, grinning. Oliver's enthusiasm was infectious, and she felt her own excitement building. This was why she'd started this journey— to capture these stories, to understand how food connected families and communities across generations.

The kitchen, when she found it twenty minutes later, was the heart of the house in every sense. A massive stone fireplace dominated one wall, with copper pots hanging from hooks above. A large wooden table sat in the center, scarred by decades of use and currently laden with the evidence of serious cooking: bowls of fresh pasta, jars of preserved vegetables, and loaves of bread that were still warm from the oven.

Three people looked up as she entered, and Sofia immediately rose to make introductions.

"Sophie, please let me introduce you to everyone," she said, gesturing first to an elderly man seated at the head of the table. "This is my grandfather, Marco De Luca—*Nonno* to everyone who knows him."

Marco was perhaps in his eighties, but his eyes were sharp and intelligent, set in a face weathered by decades of sun and wind. His hands, Sophie noticed, bore the calluses and scars of a lifetime working the land, yet they moved with surprising grace as he set down his espresso cup and rose to greet her.

"*Benvenuta*, Sophie," he said, his voice carrying the warm authority of a patriarch. "Welcome to our home. Sofia tells me you understand the old ways—that you see food as more than just business."

"*Grazie*, Marco," Sophie replied, accepting his firm handshake. "I'm honored to be here. Your olive groves are the most beautiful I've ever seen."

A smile creased his weathered features. "Ah, you have good eyes. These trees, they are not just our livelihood— they are our ancestors. Some have been in our family for five generations."

Sofia gestured to a woman in her fifties with perfectly styled hair and clothes that suggested she'd be more at home in a Milan boutique than a farmhouse kitchen. "And this is Gabriella Rosso, our neighbor and dear friend. Her family owns the vineyard to the south."

Gabriella's smile was polite but somewhat reserved as she extended a manicured hand. "Welcome, Sophie. I hope you enjoy your stay in our little corner of Tuscany."

"Finally," Sofia said, indicating a man about her own age who had been quietly observing the introductions, "this is my cousin Antonio. He helps manage the business side of our operation."

Antonio was handsome in the classic Italian way—dark hair, olive skin, and eyes that seemed to take in everything without revealing his thoughts. His handshake was firm, his smile pleasant, but Sophie sensed a certain tension in his posture.

"*Piacere*, Sophie," he said. "I look forward to hearing your thoughts on our operation. Fresh eyes can be helpful... especially from someone not buried in the past."

They settled around the table, and Sofia immediately began loading Sophie's plate with local specialties: fresh ricotta drizzled with honey, thin slices of prosciutto that melted on the tongue, and bread topped with tomatoes and basil that tasted like concentrated sunshine.

"So tell us," Marco said, leaning forward with genuine interest, "what brings you to study the olive? Most American food writers want the wine, the pasta. But the olive—this is the foundation of everything we do."

Sophie sipped the robust red wine Antonio had poured for her, considering her words. "I think Americans are just beginning to understand what you've known for centuries—that the way we produce our food matters. It's not just about taste, though your olive oil obviously tastes incredible. It's about sustainability, about preserving traditions that connect us to the land."

Marco's eyes lit up. "*Esatto*! Exactly! You see, the olive tree, she teaches patience. You cannot rush her, cannot force her to produce more than she wants to give. She rewards those who understand her rhythms, who work with nature instead of against it."

"*Nonno* gets philosophical about the olives," Antonio

said with what might have been affection or mild exasperation. "But the reality is that traditional methods are expensive, time-consuming. Other producers in the region have modernized, increased yields—"

"And lost their souls," Marco interrupted sharply. "What good is more oil if it tastes like nothing? If it comes from trees that are fed chemicals and treated like machines instead of living beings?"

The tension that Sophie had sensed earlier suddenly sharpened, crackling between grandfather and grandson like static electricity. Gabriella shifted uncomfortably in her seat, while Sofia jumped up to refill everyone's wine glasses with perhaps more enthusiasm than necessary.

"The market is changing, *Nonno*," Antonio continued, his voice carefully controlled. "Consumers want a consistent supply, competitive pricing. We can honor tradition while still being realistic about business."

Marco's weathered hands clenched into fists on the table. "Business, always business! And what happens when we squeeze every last euro from the land? When we forget why our ancestors planted these trees?"

Gabriella leaned forward, her tone smooth.

"Surely there's room for tradition and innovation, Marco. Perhaps Sophie can help us strike the right balance —through her blog, I mean."

She offered Sophie a tight smile that didn't quite reach her eyes.

"*Basta*," Sofia interjected firmly, setting the wine bottle down with a decisive clink. "Enough. Sophie is here to learn about our traditions, not to witness family arguments." She turned to Sophie with an apologetic smile. "I am sorry. Sometimes the passion, it runs very hot in our family."

Sophie held up a hand. "Please, don't apologize. Passion is exactly what I want to capture. These questions about tradition versus modernization—they're happening everywhere, in every culture. It's what makes food stories so compelling."

Marco studied her for a long moment, then nodded approvingly. "You understand. Good. Then tomorrow, you will come with me to the grove at sunrise. I will show you how we have done things for two hundred years. You will taste the difference that patience makes."

"I would be honored," Sophie replied sincerely.

The conversation turned to lighter topics—the upcoming harvest festival, local food traditions, Sofia's plans to expand their agriturismo offerings. But Sophie remained aware of the undercurrents, the way Antonio's jaw tightened whenever Marco spoke about tradition, the way Gabriella seemed to watch the family dynamics with more than casual interest.

As the evening wound down and the others began to clear the table, Marco caught Sophie's arm gently.

"*Signorina*," he said quietly, "there are things about this land that go deeper than olive trees. Stories that have been buried for generations. Some secrets, they have roots that go very deep."

Before Sophie could ask what he meant, Sofia appeared at his elbow.

"*Nonno*, you are tired. And Sophie needs rest after her journey. The stories can wait."

Marco looked like he wanted to say more, but he

simply nodded and kissed Sophie's cheek. "*Buonanotte, cara*. Sleep well."

Later, as Sophie prepared for bed, she found herself thinking about Marco's cryptic words. Standing at her window, looking out over the moonlit olive groves, she could see why people might develop almost mystical feelings about this place. The ancient trees seemed to whisper secrets to each other in the night breeze, their silver leaves catching the light like scattered coins.

Her phone buzzed with a final message from Nate back in California.

> Nate: Hope you made it to Italy safely. Can't wait to hear about the olive oil adventures. Take care of yourself. 🩶

Sophie smiled, warmth spreading through her chest. Three months ago, the idea of someone caring about her travels would have felt foreign. Now, it felt like coming home to something she hadn't realized she'd been missing.

> Sophie: Safe and sound in the most beautiful place you can imagine. I'll call you tomorrow and tell you everything. Miss you.

As she drifted off to sleep, Sophie found herself already planning her blog post about the De Luca family. But Marco's words echoed in her mind: "*This land hides more than olives. The soil remembers.*"

Tomorrow, she would learn what the soil remembered. Tonight, she slept peacefully, unaware that somewhere in the grove below her window, secrets lay buried beneath an ancient stone, waiting for the right moment to bloom into something far more dangerous than she could imagine.

———————

FROM SOPHIE'S SUBSTACK: *Farm-to-Table Adventures*

"*Arrived at the De Luca agriturismo today, and I'm already falling in love with Tuscany. There's something about olive groves that speaks to the soul—these twisted, ancient trees that have weathered centuries of change while remaining steadfast in their purpose. Tomorrow I begin learning about traditional olive oil production from Marco De Luca, whose family has been working this land for two hundred years. But I suspect there's more buried in this soil than fruit...*"

CHAPTER 2
ROOTS AND TENSIONS

THE ROOSTER'S crow pierced the pre-dawn darkness like a rusty blade, pulling Sophie from dreams filled with ancient stones and whispered warnings. She'd slept fitfully, her mind churning over Marco's cryptic words and the strange feeling of being watched in the grove. Now, as pale light crept through her shutters, she felt a thrill of anticipation. Today, she would learn the secrets of olive oil production that had been passed down through two centuries of De Luca hands.

She dressed quickly in jeans and a wool sweater, then pulled on the sturdy boots she'd brought for vineyard work. The house was still quiet as she made her way downstairs, but the kitchen already carried the warm scent of fresh coffee and baking bread. Marco sat at the wooden table, cradling an espresso cup in his weathered hands, fully dressed despite the early hour.

"*Buongiorno*, Sophie," he said, his eyes bright with the alertness of someone who'd spent a lifetime rising before the sun. "You are ready to meet the trees?"

"More than ready," Sophie replied, accepting the cup of dark, aromatic coffee Sofia placed in her hands. The liquid was strong enough to wake the dead, with a bitter edge that spoke of beans roasted to perfection.

"*Bene!* Then we go before the world wakes up. The olives, they speak most clearly in the quiet hours."

They stepped out into the crisp October morning, their breath visible in small puffs. The landscape was transformed by dawn—what had seemed mysterious and shadowed the night before now revealed itself in shades of silver and gold. Dew clung to every surface, turning spider webs into jeweled masterpieces and making the olive leaves shimmer like scattered coins.

Marco moved through the grove with the confident stride of someone who could navigate these paths blindfolded. He carried a gnarled wooden walking stick, worn smooth by decades of use, and Sophie noticed how he paused occasionally to touch a tree trunk or examine the ground at its base—gestures so automatic they seemed unconscious.

"This section," he said, stopping beside a group of particularly ancient trees, "these are our *nonnas*—our grandmothers. Five hundred years old, some of them. See how their trunks twist? Each scar tells a story of drought survived, storms weathered, generations who cared for them."

Sophie raised her camera, but Marco held up a hand.

"First, you taste," he said, reaching up to pluck an olive from a low branch. "Here. Tell me what you discover."

The olive was firm between Sophie's teeth, the flesh slightly bitter with an underlying complexity that reminded her of the terroir she'd learned to appreciate in wine. But there was something else—a depth of flavor that seemed to carry the essence of the soil itself.

"It tastes like... history," she said finally, surprising herself with the answer.

Marco's weathered face creased into a smile. "*Esatto!* You understand. This is not just fruit—this is time made tangible. Every olive carries the story of rain that fell, sunshine that warmed, hands that tended."

As they walked deeper into the grove, Marco began to explain the traditional methods his family had used for generations. How they watched the olives change color from green to purple-black, determining the perfect moment for harvest. How they still picked by hand, preserving the fruit's integrity in ways that mechanical harvesters couldn't match.

"The machines, they are fast, *sì*," Marco said, his voice carrying a note of disdain. "But they shake the trees like earthquakes. They take the fruit whether it is ready or not, bruise the olives, and let them oxidize. What we gain in speed, we lose in soul."

"But surely some modernization helps?" Sophie asked carefully, thinking of Antonio's comments the night before. "Better storage, temperature control?"

Marco's expression darkened. "Ah, you sound like my grandson. Always pushing, always wanting to change what has worked for two hundred years." He struck the ground with his walking stick for emphasis. "Tell me, if we abandon our methods, what separates us from the factories? What makes our oil special?"

Before Sophie could answer, the sound of approaching footsteps made them both turn. A man was walking toward them through the grove—tall, lean, with the sun-weathered skin of someone who worked outdoors. He wore work clothes and boots caked with soil, and something in his posture suggested he belonged here as much as the trees themselves.

But the moment Marco saw him, the old man's entire demeanor changed. His shoulders stiffened, his jaw set in hard lines, and his grip tightened on his walking stick until his knuckles went white.

"Paolo," Marco said, the name carrying the weight of old grievances.

"Marco." The word came out soft, but edged. "Out surveying the kingdom before sunrise?"

"This is my land," Marco replied sharply. "I walk where I choose, when I choose."

Paolo Bianchi—for Sophie realized this must be the neighboring olive farmer Sofia had mentioned—was perhaps sixty, with silver threading through his dark hair and intelligent eyes that seemed to take in everything without revealing his thoughts. His presence radiated a quiet authority that spoke of his own connection to the land.

"*Certo*, of course," Paolo said with studied politeness. "I was only checking the boundary near the old stone. The recent rains have caused some erosion."

"The boundary is clear," Marco snapped. "It has been clear for fifty years."

Sophie felt the tension crackling between the two men like static electricity before a storm. Whatever had happened between them ran deeper than neighborly disputes over property lines.

"And you are?" Paolo asked, turning to Sophie with what seemed like genuine curiosity.

"Sophie Brooks," she replied, extending her hand. "I'm here documenting traditional olive oil production for my food blog."

Paolo's handshake was firm, his smile more natural than anything she'd seen from him so far. "Ah, the American writer. Sofia mentioned you were coming. Welcome to our little corner of Tuscany."

"Paolo owns the grove to the east," Marco said grudgingly. "He has... different ideas about tradition."

A shadow of something—pain? regret?—flashed across Paolo's features. "We all adapt as we must, Marco. The world changes whether we wish it or not."

"Some things should not change," Marco replied fiercely. "Some things are worth preserving, no matter the cost."

Paolo studied the older man for a long moment, his expression unreadable. "Yes," he said quietly. "Some things are. But determining what those things are... that is where we differ."

He turned back to Sophie, his manner brightening artificially. "I hope you will visit our operation as well, *signorina*. We have embraced some modern techniques that might interest you. Not everything old is automatically better, despite what some believe."

With that parting shot, he touched his cap in a gesture that might have been respectful or mocking, and walked away through the trees. Sophie watched him go, noting how he moved with the same easy familiarity as Marco—a man who knew these paths as well as his own heartbeat.

"What was that about?" Sophie asked once Paolo was out of earshot.

Marco's jaw worked as if he were chewing something

bitter. "Old wounds," he said finally. "Some cuts never heal properly, especially when salt keeps being rubbed in them."

"Salt?"

"He took something from us once," Marco said, his voice heavy with old anger. "Something that cannot be replaced, cannot be forgiven. He knows what he did, and he knows I know. That is enough."

They continued walking, but the encounter had cast a pall over the morning's magic. Marco's explanations became more clipped, his movements more agitated. When they reached the irrigation system, he pointed out the traditional methods of water distribution with less enthusiasm than before.

It was Sophie who noticed the damaged line. She hesitated. It could have been age, animals, anything—but the tear looked... too neat.

"Marco, look at this," she said, crouching beside the torn tubing she'd spotted the day before. "This looks deliberate."

Marco knelt beside her, his weathered fingers tracing the ragged edges. "*Madonna mia*," he breathed. "This is not wear, not accident. Someone has cut this."

The damage was extensive—water had been seeping for hours, perhaps all night, creating a muddy mess around the base of one of the ancient trees. Marco's face grew darker as he examined the site, his anger building like a storm gathering strength.

"Paolo," he muttered. "First he destroys my family, now he sabotages my trees."

"Do you really think he would do something like this?" Sophie asked, though even as she spoke, she remembered the tension between the two men, the weight of whatever grievance lay between them.

"Who else knows these groves well enough to move through them unseen? Who else has reason to want my operation to fail?" Marco's voice rose with each word. "He pretends to be concerned about boundaries, but I know what he is really doing. He is trying to force me to sell, to give up what my family has built."

Sophie photographed the damage, her mind working through the implications. If Paolo was behind this, it represented a serious escalation in whatever conflict existed between the neighbors. But something about the deliberate nature of the cut troubled her—it seemed almost too obvious, too easy to blame on an obvious suspect.

"Should we report this to the police?" she asked.

Marco shook his head firmly. "What would they do? Paolo has friends in town, influence. They would say it was wear and tear, or animals. No, we handle this ourselves, as we always have."

They spent the next hour repairing the damaged line, Marco's movements sharp with suppressed fury. As they worked, he told Sophie about the history of his family's land, the generations who had worked these same trees, the traditions passed down from father to son.

"We came here with nothing but knowledge and determination," he said, wrapping tape around the repaired tubing. "My great-great-grandfather planted the first trees with his own hands, cleared the terraces stone by stone. This soil is mixed with De Luca blood and sweat."

"And Paolo's family?" Sophie asked carefully.

Marco's expression darkened further. "The Bianchis have been here almost as long. Once, our families were close—friends, almost like brothers. Our children played together, we shared equipment during harvest, helped each other through difficult seasons."

"What changed?"

Marco straightened slowly, his back creaking with the effort. For a long moment, he stared out over the grove, his eyes distant with painful memories.

"My son," he said finally, his voice barely above a whisper. "Paolo's daughter. Young love, foolish hearts. But families, they had different ideas about suitable matches. Words were spoken that could not be taken back. Choices were made that destroyed more than just romance."

Sophie waited, sensing there was more to the story, but Marco had closed off, his face shuttering like windows being slammed against a storm.

"That was long ago," he said firmly. "But some betrayals echo through generations. Paolo knows what he cost my family. He knows why I can never forgive."

They walked back toward the farmhouse in silence, the earlier magic of the morning completely dissipated. Sophie's mind churned with questions—about the sabotage, about the history between the families, about the weight of secrets that seemed to hang over this beautiful place like morning mist.

As they approached the house, she could see Sofia and Antonio in the courtyard, their heads bent together in what appeared to be an intense conversation. When they spotted Marco and Sophie, they quickly separated, but not before Sophie caught the tension in their postures.

"*Buongiorno,*" Sofia called out, but her smile seemed forced. "How was your walk?"

"Educational," Marco replied grimly. "Someone

damaged our irrigation system during the night. Cut the lines deliberately."

Antonio straightened, his expression sharpening. "Sabotage? Are you certain?"

"The cuts were clean, purposeful. This was not an accident."

Sophie watched Antonio's face carefully, noting how his jaw tightened with what might have been anger—or guilt. His eyes flicked toward the grove, then back to his grandfather.

"Do you suspect anyone in particular?" Antonio asked, his voice carefully neutral.

"I have my ideas," Marco replied darkly. "But accusations without proof only lead to more trouble."

Sofia wrapped her arms around herself, though the morning wasn't particularly cold. "This is terrible. Why would someone want to hurt our operation?"

"Because," Marco said heavily, "there are people who would benefit if we were forced to sell. People who see dollar signs instead of heritage when they look at our land."

Over a late breakfast of fresh bread, local cheese, and oil from the previous year's harvest, the conversation remained subdued. Sophie found herself studying each family member, wondering about alliances and motivations. Antonio seemed genuinely upset about the sabotage, but there was something in his manner that suggested he wasn't entirely surprised. Sofia appeared worried but distracted, as if her mind was on other concerns.

"What's our security situation?" Antonio asked as they finished eating. "Do we have cameras in the grove?"

Marco snorted. "Cameras! As if I would turn our home

into a prison. We have neighbors, we have trust—or we used to. That should be enough."

"Maybe it's time to reconsider," Antonio pressed. "If someone is actively trying to sabotage our operation—"

"No." Marco's voice carried the finality of granite. "I will not live in fear on my own land. We will increase our vigilance, watch for strangers. But we will not hide behind machines."

After breakfast, Sophie excused herself to process the morning's events and update her blog. In her room, she spread out the photos she'd taken—the beautiful grove at dawn, the ancient trees, and the damning evidence of sabotage. But it was the image of Paolo and Marco facing off that held her attention longest. Even captured in a still photograph, the tension between them was palpable.

Her phone buzzed with a message from Oliver.

> Oliver: Darling, how goes the olive oil adventure? Please tell me you're not just taking pretty pictures of trees. I need drama, passion, maybe a handsome Italian farmer or two! 🫒❚❚

Sophie typed back quickly:

> Sophie: Plenty of drama, though not the romantic kind. Family tensions, sabotage, old grudges. Starting to feel like there's a lot more simmering under the surface here than olive oil.

> Oliver: Sabotage?! Sophie, you have the most remarkable talent for stumbling into mysteries. Are you sure you're not secretly a magnet for trouble?

> Sophie: I'm beginning to wonder that myself. But this family has been so welcoming, and their traditions are fascinating. I just hope whatever's going on doesn't escalate.

Before Oliver could respond, another notification flashed across her screen—this one from Nate. The sight of his name tugged at something deeper, steadier, than Oliver's playful banter.

> Nate: Safe out there? Been thinking about you since you left Sonoma. Wish I could see those groves myself. 🤍

Sophie smiled despite the tension knotted in her chest.

> Sophie: I'm safe. The groves are breathtaking—you'd love them. I'll tell you more tonight.

> Nate: Good. Just… trust your gut, Soph. You always know when something's off.

His words echoed Oliver's, but carried a weight all their own. She slipped the phone back into her pocket, warmed by the thought that two very different voices in her life believed in her instincts.

> Oliver: Just promise me you'll be careful. And take notes—this sounds like material for a novel, not just a blog post!

As Sophie set her phone aside, she found herself staring out at the grove again. The morning's beauty seemed shadowed now by the knowledge of what lay beneath—old hurts, current tensions, and someone willing to commit sabotage to achieve their goals.

Marco's warning from the night before echoed in her mind: "*Some roots grow around secrets—and choke anyone who tries to unearth them.*"

She was beginning to understand that in a place where families had lived and worked for centuries, the past wasn't just history—it was a living thing that reached into the present with gnarled fingers, shaping every relation-ship, every decision, every act of love or betrayal.

The harvest festival would begin soon, and Sofia had mentioned that the entire community would be there. Perhaps in that gathering, Sophie would begin to under-stand the complex web of relationships that connected these families—and what someone might be willing to do to protect their secrets.

But tonight, she would help Sofia prepare traditional dishes for the celebration, learning recipes that had been passed down through generations of De Luca women. Food, she had learned, often revealed truths that words could not express.

Sophie found Sofia in the kitchen, already elbow-deep in flour. A hand-cranked pasta machine clamped to the edge of the old table gleamed like a relic from another century, and the scent of garlic sautéing in olive oil filled the air like perfume.

"Ah, *perfetto!* Just in time," Sofia said, brushing a streak of flour from her cheek with the back of her hand. "You knead. I roll. Together, we feed an army."

"I've been promoted to sous-chef already?" Sophie teased, slipping on the apron Sofia tossed her.

"No, no," Sofia said, grinning. "This is a promotion to *nonna-in-training*. A much higher honor."

They worked in companionable rhythm—Sofia rolling paper-thin sheets of dough, Sophie kneading and cutting. There was something meditative about it, the old rhythm of hands moving through flour and memory.

"My mother taught me this recipe," Sofia said quietly after a while. "But it was *Nonna Luisa* who taught her. She had a way of knowing when dough was ready just by the sound it made under her palms."

"That's beautiful," Sophie said. "Like the trees."

"Exactly," Sofia nodded, then added softly, "Everything here is alive with memory. Sometimes I think the kitchen knows more about us than we know about each other."

Sophie hesitated before speaking. "Do you think Marco's right about Paolo? That he would actually sabotage the grove?"

Sofia's hands didn't pause, but her eyes flicked up briefly—just long enough for Sophie to register the hesitation.

"I think..." Sofia began, shaping ravioli with practiced fingers, "that grief makes men see ghosts. Especially when there's guilt tangled up in it."

"Guilt?"

Sofia's jaw tightened. She turned back to her dough, voice lighter now. "*Basta*, enough of that. We focus on the food. You want to make Nonna proud, yes?"

Sophie didn't press. The shift in tone was clear—a door quietly closing. But she couldn't ignore the sense that Sofia was holding back more than recipes.

Still, as they filled the ravioli with fresh ricotta and sage, Sophie felt something familiar stir in her chest—not suspicion this time, but connection. Whatever secrets this family carried, they were wrapped in love and tradition too. And sometimes, the truth revealed itself not through confrontation, but through what people chose not to say.

---

*FROM SOPHIE'S SUBSTACK: **Farm-to-Table Adventures***

"This morning I learned that olive oil production is about more than pressing fruit — it's about preserving a way of life that connects families to the land across generations. But I also discovered that in places where tradition runs deep, change can feel like betrayal. When old wounds refuse to heal, even paradise has roots deep enough to trip you if you're not watching your step."

CHAPTER 3
THE DEVELOPER'S SMILE

AS THE SUN reached its zenith over the Tuscan hills, Paolo Bianchi stood among his olive trees, his weathered hands trembling slightly as he pressed the phone to his ear. The grove around him whispered with centuries of secrets, but the words he spoke now would add a new chapter to the region's complicated history.

"*Pronto,* Vincenzo? *Sì,* it is done. The irrigation line is damaged, just as we discussed." Paolo's voice carried the weight of a man who had crossed a line from which there was no return. "Marco suspects me, of course, but he has no proof. The festival is coming up—if your American friend arrives as planned, the timing will be perfect."

He listened to the response, his jaw tightening with each word from the other end. "*No,* I do not like this any more than you do. But the old man will never sell willingly, and my family... we cannot wait much longer. Do what you must, but remember our agreement. When this is over, the Bianchi name will still be carved into this land. That's all I care about."

Paolo ended the call and stood for a long moment among trees his grandfather had planted, their gnarled branches reaching toward a sky that seemed suddenly less blue. What he was about to set in motion would change everything—for the De Lucas, for himself, and for the American food blogger who did not know she was about to become a pawn in a game that had been decades in the making.

TWENTY MINUTES LATER, Sophie Brooks climbed into Sofia's small Fiat for the drive to Montepulciano's weekly market, blissfully unaware of the forces aligning against the De Luca family. The morning's encounter with Paolo still troubled her, but the prospect of exploring the local market and meeting more of the community filled her with excitement.

"You will love the market," Sofia said as they wound down the hill toward town. "Thursday is the big day— farmers come from all over the region. And the food..." She kissed her fingertips in the universal Italian gesture of perfection. "You will taste things that make you understand why we fight so hard to preserve our traditions."

The market sprawled across Montepulciano's main piazza, a riot of colors, scents, and sounds that assaulted the senses in the most delightful way. Vendors called out their wares in rapid Italian, their voices mixing with the laughter of children and the heated discussions of local housewives debating the merits of different olive oils. The autumn air carried the perfume of ripe fruit, aged cheese, and the wood smoke from a vendor grilling sausages over an open flame.

Sophie moved through the stalls with her camera, capturing the vibrant displays of produce that spoke to the region's agricultural richness. Purple eggplants gleamed like jewels beside baskets of late-season tomatoes, their skins still warm from yesterday's sun. Wheels of pecorino cheese sat in neat pyramids, their surfaces dusted with herbs and showing the careful craftsmanship of generations of cheese makers.

"*Signora Sofia!*" A cheerful voice called out. Sophie turned to see Elena Costa waving from behind a stall overflowing with specialty foods. Elena was perhaps fifty, with graying hair pinned back in a practical bun and eyes that sparkled with intelligence and warmth. Her stall was a carefully curated collection of local delicacies: honey in glass jars that caught the light like amber, bottles of olive oil in various shades of green and gold, and wheels of cheese that promised flavors developed over months of careful aging.

"*Buongiorno*, Elena," Sofia replied, leading Sophie over to the stall. "Elena runs the best specialty food shop in the region. If you want to understand Tuscan cuisine, she is the person to talk to."

She studied Sophie for a moment, her eyes sharp despite her smile.

"You write about food," Elena said, tilting her head slightly. "But can you taste its story?"

She produced a small piece of bread and drizzled it with olive oil from an unmarked bottle.

"This is from my cousin's grove—they still use

methods from the Middle Ages. Taste, and tell me what you think."

Sophie took a bite, and her eyes widened. The oil was unlike anything she'd experienced—peppery and complex, with notes that seemed to change on her tongue. There was an earthiness that spoke of ancient soil, a fruitiness that captured the essence of perfect olives, and a finish that lingered like a promise.

"This is incredible," Sophie said honestly. "The depth of flavor is extraordinary."

Elena beamed with pride. "This is what we fight to preserve. Not just the taste, but the knowledge, the connection to the land. When I see what some producers are doing now—rushing the process, using chemicals, treating olives like a commodity instead of a gift from the earth—it breaks my heart."

"Is that a widespread problem?" Sophie asked, pulling out her notebook.

Elena's expression grew troubled. "More than we like to admit. There are pressures—economic, political. Some families are struggling to maintain traditional methods. The temptation to modernize, to increase yields..." She shrugged eloquently. "Not everyone can resist."

As they talked, Sophie became aware of a man watching them from across the piazza. He was perhaps forty-five, impeccably dressed in a way that suggested city money, his dark hair perfectly styled despite the morning's breeze. Something about his focused attention made her uncomfortable—he wasn't browsing the market like other visitors, but seemed specifically interested in their conversation.

"Elena," Sofia said quietly, following Sophie's gaze, "Vincenzo is here."

Elena's face immediately tightened, her earlier warmth replaced by wariness. "So I see. I wonder what brings him to market day."

The man—Vincenzo—began walking toward them with the confident stride of someone accustomed to getting what he wanted. His smile was perfectly calibrated, friendly but somehow predatory, like a shark in expensive clothing.

"Sofia, *bella*," he said, arriving at the stall with arms spread in an exaggerated gesture of friendship. "How lovely to see you. And you must be the American food writer I've heard so much about."

Sophie found herself shaking hands with Vincenzo, immediately noting the manicured nails and soft palms of someone who'd never done manual labor. His cologne was expensive but applied with a heavy hand, as if he needed to mask something unpleasant underneath.

"Vincenzo Rossi," he said, holding her hand slightly longer than necessary. "I develop luxury properties in the region. Perhaps you'd be interested in seeing what modern Tuscany can offer—resort accommodations, world-class restaurants, spa facilities that rival anything in Milan."

"Thank you," Sophie replied carefully, "but I'm specifically here to document traditional agricultural methods. Family operations like the De Lucas."

Something flickered behind Vincenzo's polished smile —annoyance, perhaps, or calculation. "Ah, yes, the De Lucas. Such a charming family, so... dedicated to their old ways. Though I do worry about their long-term viability. Marco is getting on in years, and the younger generation seems more realistic about the challenges facing traditional farming."

Sophie caught the subtle emphasis on "realistic" and the way Sofia's spine stiffened at the words. This was clearly not the first time Vincenzo had made such comments.

"Antonio is a smart boy," Vincenzo continued smoothly. "He understands that preserving tradition doesn't have to mean rejecting progress. There are ways to honor the past while embracing the future—ways that could benefit everyone involved."

"What exactly do you mean?" Sophie asked, though she suspected she already knew.

Vincenzo's smile widened, revealing teeth that were too white and too perfect. "Simply that land is a resource, not a museum piece. The De Luca property has tremendous potential—imagine a luxury resort where guests could experience authentic Tuscan life while enjoying modern amenities. Traditional olive groves preserved as landscaping, historic buildings converted to premium accommodations. Everyone wins."

Elena made a small sound of disgust. "Everyone except the families who have worked this land for centuries. Everyone except the traditions that make this region special."

"*Cara Elena,*" Vincenzo said, his tone condescending despite the endearment, "sentiment doesn't pay the bills. How many young people are staying to work the olive groves? How many families can afford to maintain traditional methods when industrial operations can produce oil at a fraction of the cost?"

"Perhaps," Elena replied sharply, "because people like

you keep buying up properties and turning them into playgrounds for wealthy tourists instead of supporting the families who make this region authentic."

The tension crackled between them, and Sophie sensed this was an argument that had been playing out across the region for years—tradition versus development, preservation versus profit.

"I simply offer options," Vincenzo said with practiced reasonableness. "If families choose to sell, that's their decision. If they choose to partner with developers who can help them modernize while preserving their heritage, even better. The market will decide what survives and what doesn't."

Sofia had remained silent during this exchange, but Sophie could see the anger building behind her controlled expression. When she finally spoke, her voice was tight with barely suppressed fury.

"Some things are worth more than money, Vincenzo. Some things shouldn't be decided by markets."

"Of course," Vincenzo replied smoothly. "But idealism doesn't feed families or pay for Marco's medical expenses when his arthritis gets worse. It doesn't cover the cost of new equipment when the old machinery breaks down. Sometimes being practical is the kindest thing we can do for people we care about."

With that perfectly calculated parting shot, he touched his hat to the ladies and walked away, leaving behind the lingering scent of expensive cologne and implied threats.

"*Che bastardo,*" Elena muttered under her breath.

Sofia's hands were shaking slightly as she watched Vincenzo's retreating figure. "He knows exactly what to say to make you doubt yourself. Marco's arthritis, the equipment costs—these are real concerns. But the way he uses them, like weapons..."

"Has he approached your family directly?" Sophie asked.

"Many times," Sofia replied. "Always with a different offer, always with more money. And always when Marco is having a difficult day, when the pain is bad, or when something has gone wrong with the operation."

Sophie thought about yesterday morning's sabotage, the cut irrigation lines that would cost time and money to repair properly. The timing seemed too convenient to be coincidental.

"Does he have support in the community?" she asked.

Elena and Sofia exchanged a meaningful look. "More than we'd like to admit," Elena said finally. "Vincenzo is very good at finding people's pressure points. Business owners who need development to bring in tourists, families struggling with debt, even young people who see no future in traditional farming. He makes them believe that progress requires abandoning the past."

They spent another hour in the market, but the encounter with Vincenzo had cast a shadow over the morning's pleasure. Sophie found herself studying the other vendors, wondering who might be allies and who might have been swayed by the developer's promises.

As they prepared to leave, Elena pressed a bottle of the exceptional olive oil into Sophie's hands. "For your writing," she said. "So you can taste what we're fighting to preserve. And Sophie? Be careful. Vincenzo doesn't like it when outsiders interfere with his plans. The last journalist who wrote critically about development in the region had some very unfortunate experiences."

On the drive back to the agriturismo, Sofia was uncharacteristically quiet, her knuckles white as she gripped the steering wheel. Sophie had learned to recognize the signs of someone wrestling with difficult decisions.

"Sofia," she said gently, "is there something you're not telling me about the family's situation?"

Sofia was silent for so long that Sophie thought she wouldn't answer. Finally, as they turned into the drive leading to the farmhouse, she spoke.

"*Nonno* would never forgive me if he knew I was even thinking about it," she said quietly. "But Vincenzo is right about some things. The medical expenses, the equipment costs, the declining profits as we compete with industrial operations... Sometimes I wonder if we're fighting a war we can't win."

"And Antonio?"

"Antonio thinks we should at least listen to Vincenzo's offers. Not to sell completely, but to explore partnerships that might let us modernize while keeping some traditional elements. He says we can preserve the heart while updating the methods."

Sophie could hear the doubt in Sofia's voice, the exhaustion of carrying burdens that felt too heavy. "What do you think?"

"I think," Sofia said as they pulled up to the house, "that some things, once lost, can never be recovered. And I think Vincenzo Rossi understands that better than anyone —which is why he's so dangerous."

As they unloaded their market purchases, Sophie's phone buzzed with an unexpected message. The sender's name made her heart skip a beat: Ryan.

Ryan: Surprise! I'm in Italy on business and thought I'd swing by Tuscany to see how you're doing. I know things ended badly between us, but I'd love to talk. Maybe we could meet for dinner tonight? I'm staying at the Hotel Panorama in Montepulciano.

Sophie stared at the message, emotions churning through her like storm clouds. Ryan here, now, just as she was beginning to feel settled and confident in her new life? The timing felt too coincidental, too convenient. She thought of the months she'd spent clawing her way out of the wreckage of their marriage, the lies about Golden State Produce, the hollow apologies. They weren't partners anymore—legally or emotionally. So why was he here, in Tuscany of all places?

Her stomach dropped, not with fear, exactly—but with that old reflex that came from years of walking on eggshells.

"Everything okay?" Sofia asked, noticing her expression.

"My ex-husband is in town," Sophie said, still processing the shock. "He wants to meet for dinner."

Sofia raised an eyebrow. "Ex-husband? This is unexpected, no?"

"Very unexpected," Sophie replied grimly. "Ryan doesn't do anything without a reason. I'm just not sure what that reason is yet."

Her phone buzzed again, this time with a message from Oliver.

> Oliver: Darling, please tell me you're not falling for some charming Italian farmer. I need my vicarious romance to come with proper warning labels! 🍸 🩶

Despite everything, Sophie smiled. If only Oliver knew that romance was the least of her concerns right now. Between family feuds, development pressure, irrigation sabotage, and now Ryan's mysterious appearance, her quiet documentation of olive oil traditions was becoming far more complicated than she'd ever imagined.

> Sophie: No Italian farmers in my bed, I promise. But my ex-husband just showed up unexpectedly, and I have a feeling this trip is about to get a lot more interesting.

> Oliver: Ex-husband?! Sophie, darling, that's either deliciously dramatic or absolutely terrible. Please tell me you're not going to fall for whatever nonsense he's peddling.

> Sophie: I'm not that foolish anymore. But I am curious about what brought him here. It's too coincidental to be random.

> Oliver: Trust your instincts, love. They haven't steered you wrong yet. And remember—you don't owe him anything, not even politeness.

As Sophie tucked her phone away, she found herself thinking about trust, instincts, and the web of relationships that seemed to grow more complex with each passing hour. In her room, she could see workers in the olive grove, tiny figures moving among the ancient trees. Somewhere out there, secrets were buried beneath centuries of tradition and family loyalty.

Tomorrow was the harvest festival, when the entire community would gather to celebrate another successful season. But Sophie was beginning to suspect that not everyone would be celebrating—and that some people might be willing to go to extraordinary lengths to get what they wanted.

---

*From Sophie's Substack: **Farm-to-Table Adventures***

"Today I met two very different forces shaping Tuscany's future: Elena Costa, who preserves traditional foods with fierce dedication, and Vincenzo Rossi, who sees opportunity where others see heritage. The conversation between tradition and progress isn't academic here—it's playing out in real time, with real families caught in the balance. Sometimes preservation requires fighting battles you never wanted to fight..."

CHAPTER 4
WHISPERS IN THE GROVE

THE AFTERNOON SUN cast long shadows through the olive groves as Marco led Sophie down a path she hadn't walked before—narrower, older, winding through trees that seemed even more ancient than those near the house. His walking stick tapped a steady rhythm against the stone-littered earth, and Sophie noticed how his weathered hands traced the bark of certain trees as they passed, as if greeting old friends.

"This section," Marco said, pausing beside a grove that seemed somehow different from the rest, "this is where the trouble began. And where, perhaps, it will end."

The trees here were magnificent specimens, their trunks thick as wine barrels and twisted into fantastic shapes that spoke of centuries weathering wind and storm. But what caught Sophie's attention was the boundary marker at the grove's edge—not the modern concrete posts that dotted most of the property, but an ancient stone similar to the one she'd discovered the day before.

"The old boundary," Marco explained, settling onto a wooden bench that had been placed to take advantage of the view across the valley. "This stone has marked the edge of De Luca land for over three hundred years. My ancestor carved those symbols himself—see there, the olive branches intertwined with our family crest."

Sophie knelt beside the limestone marker, running her fingers over the worn carvings. The craftsmanship was exquisite, even weathered by time. The olive branches seemed to dance around symbols that might have been letters or numbers, though erosion had made them difficult to decipher.

"It's beautiful," she said honestly. "What's the significance of this particular boundary?"

Marco's expression darkened, and he struck the ground with his walking stick. "Twenty hectares of the finest olive trees in Tuscany. Soil that drains perfectly, slopes that catch the morning sun and shed the afternoon heat. My great-grandfather called it 'God's own grove.' It should have been passed to my son, and from him to his children."

"Should have been?"

"The Bianchi family has contested this boundary for fifty years," Marco said, his voice heavy with old anger. "They claim these twenty hectares were stolen from them generations ago, that the original survey markers were moved in the night by my ancestors. They have produced documents, witnesses, lawyers. Always lawyers."

Sophie thought about Paolo's tense demeanor that morning, the way he'd mentioned checking the boundary after recent rains. "Do they have legitimate grounds for their claim?"

Marco was quiet for a long moment, his eyes fixed on

the disputed grove. When he finally spoke, his voice carried the weight of old sorrows.

"In 1943, during the war, many records were lost. Bombed, burned, simply disappeared in the chaos. The Bianchis claim they had documents proving their ownership, but those papers were destroyed when the Germans retreated through the valley. All that remained were memory, tradition, and these stones."

"And your family's position?"

"This stone was placed by my ancestor's hand. These trees were planted by De Luca sweat. For three centuries, our family has worked this soil, paid taxes on this land, been buried beneath these olive branches." Marco's voice rose with each word. "How can papers that conveniently disappeared prove what these stones have witnessed for generations?"

As they talked, Sophie became aware of a sound that didn't belong—the steady thud of footsteps approaching through the grove. Marco heard it too, his posture straightening with wariness.

"Paolo," he muttered. "I should have known he would come sniffing around after this morning's encounter."

But it wasn't Paolo who emerged from between the trees. It was Antonio, and his face carried an expression Sophie hadn't seen before—guilt mixed with defiance, like a child caught in an act of rebellion.

"*Nonno*," he said, stopping when he saw Sophie. "I didn't expect to find you here."

"This is still my land," Marco replied sharply. "I walk where I choose. What brings you to the disputed grove, grandson?"

Antonio's gaze flicked between Marco and Sophie,

clearly uncomfortable with having an audience for whatever conversation he'd planned. "I wanted to check the
trees before tomorrow's festival. Make sure everything is
ready for the demonstration you planned."

It was a reasonable explanation, but something in
Antonio's manner suggested there was more to the story.
His clothes showed signs of exertion—sweat stains, dirt on
his shoes that looked fresh. And unless Sophie was
mistaken, that was the scent of expensive cologne clinging
to his shirt, the same overpowering fragrance Vincenzo
had worn that morning.

"The trees are ready," Marco said, his eyes narrowing as
he studied his grandson. "They have been ready for weeks.
What is this really about, Antonio?"

Antonio's eyes flicked—just for a moment—toward the
boundary stone at the edge of the grove.

"Just family business," he said, too quickly.

The words hung in the air like an accusation. Marco's
jaw worked silently for a moment before he spoke again.

"*Sì*, family business. The kind that requires meeting
with developers in secret? The kind that involves discussions of progress and modernization behind an old man's
back?"

Antonio's face flushed, confirming what Sophie had
already suspected. "How did you—?"

"I may be old, but I am not blind," Marco snapped.
"Did you think I wouldn't notice the expensive car
parked at the crossroads? Did you think I wouldn't
recognize the smell of that man's cologne on your
clothes?"

Sophie felt like an intruder in this family drama, but
she was also fascinated by the dynamics playing out

before her. This was clearly a confrontation that had been building for some time.

"*Nonno*, please listen," Antonio said, his voice taking on a pleading tone. "Vincenzo has made some very reasonable proposals. We don't have to sell everything—he's talking about partnerships, joint ventures that would let us preserve the traditional elements while updating our methods."

"Partnerships," Marco spat. "With a man who sees our heritage as nothing more than marketing material for wealthy tourists. Tell me, grandson, what does he want in return for this generous partnership?"

Antonio's silence was answer enough.

"The disputed land," Marco continued remorselessly. "He wants the twenty hectares that the Bianchis have been fighting for, doesn't he? He thinks if he can get that section, he can build his resort and still claim to be preserving authentic Tuscan agriculture."

"It's not that simple," Antonio protested. "The legal situation with that land is complicated. If we could resolve the boundary dispute, it would benefit everyone. The Bianchis would get compensation, we would get clear title to the rest of the property, and Vincenzo could develop a small section while preserving the majority of the grove."

Marco stood slowly, his walking stick trembling in his grip. For a moment, Sophie thought he might strike his grandson. Instead, he turned away, staring out over the disputed grove.

"You would trade your birthright for a developer's promise," he said quietly. "You would trust a man like Vincenzo Rossi to preserve what five generations of your family have built."

"I'm trying to save our family business!" Antonio shot back. "You refuse to see that we're struggling. The medical bills, the equipment costs, the competition from industrial operations—we can't keep going the way we have been. Something has to change."

"Then we change what we can control," Marco replied fiercely. "We improve our marketing, we find new customers who value quality. We don't sell our souls to developers who will turn our life's work into a theme park."

As the argument escalated, Sophie found herself studying the disputed grove with new eyes. Twenty hectares of prime agricultural land, perfectly positioned for either olive cultivation or luxury development. Whoever controlled that section would have significant leverage over the entire valley's future.

Her attention was caught by movement near the tree line—a flash of color that didn't belong among the silver-green olive leaves. Someone was watching them, staying hidden but clearly interested in the family confrontation playing out.

Sophie stepped away from the arguing men, moving casually toward the spot where she'd seen the movement. As she pretended to photograph the ancient trees, she caught another glimpse of the watcher—a woman with dark hair, wearing a red scarf that had given her away.

Gabriella Rosso. What was their elegant neighbor doing lurking in the De Luca grove, eavesdropping on private family business?

Why was she watching from the shadows instead of approaching? Was it coincidence—or something more calculated? Gabriella adjusted her scarf with the grace of someone used to being watched—but not caught.

Sophie waited until both men had disappeared before moving toward the spot where she'd seen Gabriella. The ground showed signs of recent disturbance—footprints in the soft earth, broken twigs where someone had pushed through the underbrush. But the watcher was gone, vanished as completely as if she'd never been there.

Before Sophie could investigate further, the sound of Marco's walking stick striking the ground repeatedly brought her attention back to the confrontation.

"Enough!" the old man declared. "I will not stand here and listen to my own grandson plot the destruction of everything I have worked for. Antonio, you will end this association with Vincenzo Rossi immediately. You will tell him that the De Luca family is not interested in partnerships, joint ventures, or any other scheme he has concocted."

"And if I refuse?" Antonio challenged.

Marco's face went ashen, but his voice remained steady. "Then you are no longer my heir. Sofia will inherit the property, and you will have to find another way to make your fortune."

The threat hung in the air like a thunderclap. Antonio's defiance crumbled, replaced by shock and something that might have been fear.

"*Nonno*, you don't mean that."

"I have never been more serious about anything in my life," Marco replied. "This land is not just property—it is our family's soul. I will not see it sold to the highest bidder, no matter who does the selling."

With that, Marco turned and walked away, his walking

stick tapping an angry rhythm against the stones. Antonio stood frozen for a moment, then hurried after him, leaving Sophie alone in the disputed grove.

She waited until both men had disappeared before moving toward the spot where she'd seen Gabriella. The ground showed signs of recent disturbance—footprints in the soft earth, broken twigs where someone had pushed through the underbrush. But the watcher was gone, vanished as completely as if she'd never been there.

Sophie's phone buzzed with a message, startling her in the grove's sudden quiet.

> Ryan: I have so much to tell you about why I'm really here. Meet me at 8?

The timing of Ryan's appearance, combined with everything she'd witnessed today, sent warning bells ringing in Sophie's mind. Too many coincidences, too many people with hidden agendas converging on the De Luca family at the same time.

She typed back carefully:

> Sophie: I'll be there. But Ryan, I hope you're being honest with me about why you're in Italy.

His response came quickly:

> Ryan: More honest than I've been about anything in years. You'll understand tonight.

As Sophie made her way back toward the farm-house, her photographer's eye caught something that made her pause. Near the ancient boundary stone, someone had been digging. The disturbed earth was partially hidden by fallen leaves, but the soil was definitely darker, more recently turned than the surrounding ground.

She knelt down, brushing away the leaves to get a better look.

A shallow depression, no wider than a bread plate, had been carefully covered in leaf litter. Not deep enough for a body, but perhaps just right for a document or box...

The hole was small, carefully concealed, as if someone had buried something and then tried to hide the evidence. But what could be valuable enough to bury in such a significant location?

Before she could investigate further, the sound of approaching voices made her quickly scatter the leaves back over the disturbed earth. She straightened just as Sofia appeared on the path, accompanied by two workers carrying pruning equipment.

"Sophie!" Sofia called out. "There you are. How did you enjoy the disputed grove?"

"It's beautiful," Sophie replied honestly. "Marco told me about the boundary disputes. That must be difficult for the family."

Sofia's expression tightened. "More difficult than you know. But these are problems we must solve ourselves, as families have always done."

As they walked back together, Sofia chatting about preparations for tomorrow's festival, Sophie's mind churned with questions. Who had been digging near the boundary stone, and what had they buried? What was Gabriella doing spying on the De Luca family argument? And what role did Ryan's unexpected arrival play in the increasingly complex web of relationships surrounding the olive grove?

Back at the farmhouse, she found Marco in his study, hunched over account books with a expression of deep worry. He looked up as she entered, his weathered face showing every one of his eighty-three years.

"*Signorina*, forgive an old man's family troubles," he said wearily. "You came here to learn about olive oil, not to witness our personal dramas."

"Actually," Sophie said carefully, "I think they're more connected than you might realize. The way families manage tradition, change, and outside pressure—that's all part of the farm-to-table story."

Marco studied her with sharp eyes. "You see clearly for someone so young. *Sì*, perhaps you are right. Perhaps our personal struggles are not so personal after all."

"Marco, can I ask you something? The boundary stone in the disputed grove—has anyone been disturbing the ground around it recently?"

The old man's expression sharpened with interest. "Why do you ask?"

"I noticed some freshly turned earth nearby. Someone's been digging there recently."

Marco was quiet for a long moment, then reached into his desk drawer and withdrew a small brass key. "There are things about this property that go back further than the olive trees," he said slowly. "Things that certain people would very much like to find."

"What kind of things?"

"The kind that could resolve old disputes once and for all," Marco replied cryptically. "Or create new ones that would make the current troubles seem simple by comparison."

Before Sophie could ask more questions, Antonio appeared in the doorway, his face still flushed from his confrontation with his grandfather.

"*Nonno*, we need to talk."

Marco's expression hardened. "If you have come to apologize and promise to end your association with Vincenzo Rossi, then we can talk. Otherwise, I have nothing to say to you."

"What if I told you I might have a way to resolve the boundary dispute permanently?" Antonio asked quietly. "What if there was evidence that could prove, once and for all, who really owns the disputed land?"

Marco's grip tightened on the brass key. "What kind of evidence?"

"The kind that's been buried for seventy years," Antonio replied, his eyes fixed on his grandfather's face. "The kind that certain people would kill to keep hidden."

The words hung in the air like a death sentence, and Sophie felt a chill that had nothing to do with the approaching evening. Whatever secrets lay buried beneath the ancient boundary stone, people were willing to fight for them. The question was: how far would they go to keep those secrets from coming to light?

As the sun set over the Tuscan hills, painting the olive groves in shades of gold and shadow, Sophie prepared for her dinner with Ryan. But her mind remained focused on the mysteries surrounding the De Luca family—mysteries that seemed to grow deeper and more dangerous with each passing hour.

The town was getting ready for the harvest festival, and the entire community would gather to celebrate another successful season. But Sophie was beginning to suspect that some people might be planning a very different kind of harvest—one that had been generations in the making.

From Sophie's Substack: Farm-to-Table Adventures

"Today I learned that in places where families have worked the same land for centuries, every boundary stone tells a story. Some stories are about triumph and tradition. Others are about secrets buried so deep that people will do anything to keep them hidden. The most dangerous harvests, I'm discovering, aren't always about olives..."

CHAPTER 5
A BODY AMONG THE BRANCHES

THE HOTEL RESTAURANT was all glass walls and white linen, the kind of place that could have been anywhere in the world. It lacked the soul of the De Luca farmhouse kitchen, where even a simple loaf of bread carried generations of history. Ryan looked perfectly at home here—tailored suit, confident smile, ordering a bottle of wine without asking her preference.

The dinner with Ryan had lasted far too long and revealed far too little. He'd been charming in the same polished way that once fooled investors and customers alike—apologetic without ever admitting real fault, evasive whenever she pressed for specifics. His talk of "investment opportunities" and "reconnecting with suppliers" sounded as thin as the excuses he'd fed her back in Oregon. At one point he mentioned "emerging markets in agricultural exports," his tone a little too rehearsed, a little too slick. Sophie couldn't shake the feeling that he wasn't just here to reminisce or mend fences—he was prospecting.

Sophie had sat through it with polite detachment, the way you might endure a sales pitch you never intended to buy. By the time she left the Hotel Panorama, one truth was clear: Ryan hadn't come to Tuscany for reconciliation. He was here on business, and whatever that business was, it brushed too close to the De Luca troubles to be coincidence.

Now, as dawn light crept through her shutters, she was awakened not by the usual rooster's crow but by the sound of voices calling urgently in the courtyard below. Sofia's voice, high and strained with worry, cut through the morning air.

"*Nonno? Nonno, dove sei?*" Where are you?

Sophie threw on clothes and hurried downstairs to find Sofia and Antonio in the kitchen, both wearing expressions of deep concern. Sofia was wrapping a thick shawl around her shoulders, while Antonio paced by the window, his agitation evident in every movement.

"What's wrong?" Sophie asked, immediately alert.

"*Nonno* is missing," Sofia said, her voice tight with worry. "He always takes his morning walk through the grove at sunrise—every day for forty years, the same routine. But he didn't come back for breakfast, and we can't find him anywhere."

Antonio stopped pacing and turned to face them. "I checked the main paths, called his name. Nothing. His walking stick is gone from the door, so he definitely went out, but..." He trailed off, running a hand through his hair.

"How long has he been gone?" Sophie asked, pulling on her jacket.

"Over two hours," Sofia replied. "He's never late for breakfast. Never. Something's wrong—I can feel it."

The three of them split up to search the property more systematically. Sofia took the paths toward the house and outbuildings, Antonio headed toward the modern irrigation systems he'd been working on, and Sophie found herself drawn toward the disputed grove where she'd witnessed yesterday's confrontation.

The morning air was crisp and still, carrying the earthy scents of dew-dampened soil and the green smell of olive leaves. Sophie moved carefully along the path, calling Marco's name and listening for any response. The ancient trees seemed to watch her passage with their gnarled silence, and she couldn't shake the feeling that something was terribly wrong.

As she approached the disputed section of the grove, Sophie's photographer's eye caught something that didn't belong—a splash of color against the silver-green backdrop of the olive trees. She quickened her pace, her heart beginning to pound with a dread she couldn't quite name.

There, beneath one of the most ancient trees in the grove, lay Marco De Luca.

Sophie's breath caught in her throat as she took in the scene. Marco was sprawled at the base of the massive olive tree, his body twisted at an unnatural angle. A wooden ladder lay beside him, one of its rungs snapped cleanly in two. His walking stick was nowhere to be seen.

"*Dio mio*," Sophie whispered, rushing to his side.

She knelt beside Marco's still form, her hands trembling as she checked for a pulse she already knew she wouldn't find. His weathered skin was cold to the touch, his eyes staring sightlessly up at the olive branches that had sheltered his family for generations. Blood had pooled beneath his head, dark against the earth that had been his life's work.

Sophie forced herself to think like the investigator she'd become rather than the friend she'd grown to care for. She pulled out her phone and took photos of the scene before anything could be disturbed, her hands shaking but her mind sharp with purpose.

The ladder placement looked wrong—too far from the tree to have been useful for pruning, positioned at an angle that made no sense for someone of Marco's experience. The broken rung showed a clean break, as if it had been weakened deliberately rather than snapping under weight.

Most telling of all, Marco's walking stick was missing. In all her time with him, Sophie had never seen the old man more than arm's reach from that gnarled wooden staff. He would never have climbed a ladder without it nearby, and it certainly wouldn't have simply vanished if he'd fallen naturally.

As she circled the scene, taking more photos and noting details, Sophie's attention was caught by something that made her blood run cold. Footprints in the soft earth around the tree—boot prints that were too large and too recent to be Marco's. Someone else had been here, either with him or shortly after his death.

"Marco!" Sofia's voice carried across the grove, still calling hopefully for her grandfather.

Sophie steeled herself and called back, "Sofia! Antonio! Over here!"

The next few minutes passed in a blur of shock, grief, and desperate activity. Sofia's anguished cries when she saw her grandfather's body, Antonio's white-faced attempts to take charge of the situation, the arrival of the local emergency services with their matter-of-fact efficiency in dealing with death.

Inspector Ricci of the Carabinieri was a compact man in his fifties with intelligent eyes and the patient manner of someone who'd seen too many tragedies to be surprised by them anymore. He surveyed the scene with professional detachment while Sofia wept quietly and Antonio answered questions in a voice that never quite steadied.

"*Signor* De Luca was eighty-three years old," Inspector Ricci noted, consulting his notebook. "He had arthritis in his hands and back, yes? And he was alone this morning when he went for his walk?"

"*Sì*," Antonio confirmed. "He always walked alone at sunrise. He said it was his time to think, to plan the day's work."

"And the ladder? Was it normal for him to be pruning at this time of year?"

Sofia looked up from her grief. "No," she said firmly. "The pruning season doesn't begin until after the harvest is complete. *Nonno* would never prune now—it could damage the trees before they give up their fruit."

Inspector Ricci made a note. "Yet he climbed the ladder for some reason. Perhaps he saw something in the tree that concerned him—a diseased branch, storm damage?"

Sophie found herself speaking before she'd consciously decided to. "Inspector, I think you should look more carefully at that ladder."

Ricci turned to her with raised eyebrows. "And you are?"

"Sophie Brooks. I'm staying with the family, documenting their olive oil production methods. I found the body."

"Ah, *sì*, the American writer. What concerns you about the ladder?"

Sophie pointed to the broken rung. "That break looks too clean to be accidental. And the ladder's position—it's too far from the tree to be useful, at the wrong angle for someone trying to reach the branches."

Inspector Ricci examined the ladder more closely, his expression growing thoughtful. "You have good eyes, *signorina*. This does appear to be... unusual."

"There's something else," Sophie continued, knowing she was probably overstepping but unable to stay silent. "Marco's walking stick is missing. He never went anywhere without it, especially not when climbing ladders. And there are boot prints around the tree that don't match his shoes."

The Inspector's attention sharpened considerably. He spent the next twenty minutes examining the scene more carefully, taking photographs and measurements, instructing his team to look for the missing walking stick. Once, as he straightened from studying the prints, Sophie caught a flicker of unease in his eyes before his professional mask returned. But when he finally closed his notebook, his conclusion was disappointingly conventional.

"While there are some unusual elements," he announced to the gathered family, "the evidence suggests an accidental death. *Signor* De Luca was an elderly man with physical limitations. Perhaps he saw something in the tree that worried him—a broken branch that might fall and damage younger trees. He climbed the ladder to investigate, the rung gave way under his weight, and he fell. The missing walking stick likely rolled into the underbrush when he fell. We will search for it, but such things happen in accidents."

"What about the boot prints?" Sophie pressed.

Inspector Ricci shrugged. "Until we have something more conclusive, we must treat this as an accident. But I'll keep your observations in mind."

Sophie wanted to argue, to point out the inconsistencies that screamed murder to her trained eye. But she was a guest here, a foreigner with no official standing. And the family was drowning in grief, hardly in a position to challenge the authorities.

As the inspector's team prepared to remove Marco's body, Sofia clutched Sophie's arm with desperate strength.

"This wasn't an accident," she whispered, her voice hoarse from crying. "Someone killed him. I know it sounds crazy, but *Nonno* was too careful, too experienced to make such a mistake."

"I believe you," Sophie replied quietly. "And I'm going to find out what really happened."

Antonio, overhearing, looked stricken. "You think someone murdered him? But who would do such a thing?"

His gaze darted toward the grove before quickly shifting back. "That ladder... I don't understand. He would never use one without me helping."

Before Sophie could answer, her phone buzzed with a message. She glanced at the screen and felt her blood turn to ice.

Unknown Number: Accidents happen to people who ask too many questions. The old man learned this too late. Don't make the same mistake.

Sophie stared at the message, her hands trembling. Her thumb hovered above the screen, frozen. Whoever sent it had eyes on her—and on Marco, even in his final moments. This wasn't about olive oil anymore. It was about control. Someone had been watching, waiting, ready to threaten anyone who questioned the official story. The message confirmed what her instincts had been screaming —Marco De Luca had been murdered, and his killer was still out there.

As the morning progressed and the authorities completed their work, Sophie found herself studying everyone who came to pay their respects. Paolo Bianchi arrived with what seemed like genuine shock and sorrow, staying only long enough to offer condolences before hurrying away. Vincenzo Rossi appeared briefly, his expression appropriately solemn, but Sophie caught him glancing toward the disputed grove with what looked suspiciously like satisfaction.

Gabriella came with flowers and tears, embracing Sofia with what appeared to be sincere grief. But Sophie noticed how her eyes swept the scene, taking in details with the same calculating attention Vincenzo had shown.

Elena from the market arrived with food and fierce anger. "This is what comes of dealing with developers and their promises," she declared, loud enough for anyone nearby to hear. "Marco died fighting to preserve what mattered. Now they'll circle like vultures, trying to pick apart what he built."

As the day wore on and the family began to make funeral arrangements, Sophie retreated to her room to process what she'd learned. She spread out the photos she'd taken that morning, studying them for details she might have missed. The broken ladder rung, the missing walking stick, the suspicious boot prints—each element painted a picture of murder disguised as accident.

Sophie had documented enough rural operations to know how fiercely farmers guarded their routines—Marco's was almost ritualistic. Deviating from it meant something.

But who had the motive and opportunity to kill Marco De Luca? Antonio stood to inherit the property, but he'd seemed genuinely shocked by his grandfather's death. Paolo had a generations-old grudge, but would he really resort to murder over a boundary dispute? Vincenzo clearly wanted the land for development, but would he risk everything on such a direct approach?

And then there was Ryan, whose arrival seemed too coincidental to ignore. What "investment opportunities" had brought him to Tuscany, and did they somehow involve the De Luca property?

Sophie's phone rang, startling her from her thoughts. The caller ID showed Nate's name, and she felt a rush of relief at the prospect of hearing a friendly voice.

"Sophie, I just got your message about what happened," Nate said without preamble. "Are you okay? This sounds terrible."

"I'm okay, but Marco... Nate, I think he was murdered. The police are calling it an accident, but everything about the scene was wrong."

"Tell me what you saw."

Sophie walked Nate through her observations, from the ladder placement to the missing walking stick to the threatening text message. As she spoke, she felt some of her isolation lifting. Here was someone who understood her instincts, who didn't dismiss her concerns as the imagination of a grieving friend.

"You need to be careful," Nate said when she finished. "If someone was willing to kill Marco to protect their secrets, they won't hesitate to target anyone else who gets too close to the truth."

"I know. But I can't just walk away. This family welcomed me into their home, shared their traditions with me. I owe Marco the truth."

"Then find it," Nate replied simply. "But watch your back. And Sophie? If things get dangerous, get out. Marco wouldn't want you to become another victim in this mess."

After they hung up, Sophie sat in the gathering twilight, planning her next moves. In a few days' time, the family would gather for Marco's funeral, followed by the postponed harvest festival—a day when emotions would run high and people might reveal more than they intended.

But tonight, she had work to do. Someone had killed Marco De Luca and tried to make it look like an accident. They'd threatened her to stay silent, underestimating her determination to uncover the truth.

As darkness settled over the olive groves, Sophie prepared to begin her own harvest—gathering the secrets that had been buried too long in Tuscan soil.

The old man had died protecting his family's legacy. Now it was up to her to ensure his death hadn't been in vain.

*FROM SOPHIE'S SUBSTACK: **Farm-to-Table Adventures***

"Today I learned that some harvests yield more than fruit. Marco De Luca, who taught me that olives carry the stories of the soil, has become part of that story himself. The authorities call it an accident, but the land remembers what happened among its ancient trees. Some truths are worth dying for. Others are worth killing for. The challenge is knowing which is which..."

CHAPTER 6
MOURNING &
MANIPULATION

THE DE LUCA farmhouse had been transformed overnight into a place of mourning. Black crepe hung from the windows, and the kitchen that had been filled with laughter just days ago now hummed with the quiet efficiency of women preparing for a funeral. Sophie found herself swept into the ancient rituals of Italian grief, helping Sofia and the neighboring women prepare the traditional foods that would feed the community as they gathered to honor Marco's memory.

The work was meditative—kneading dough for bread, stirring pots of soup that would simmer for hours, arranging platters of cheese and olives with the precision of an altar. But underneath the familiar comfort of cooking, tension simmered like the broth on the stove. Everyone moved carefully around Antonio, who sat at the kitchen table surrounded by legal documents and account books, his face drawn with the weight of sudden responsibility.

"The lawyer will come to the house in a few days," he said, not looking up from the papers. "To read *Nonno's* will officially. Though we all know what it says—the property comes to me, with provisions for Sofia's care."

Sofia's hands stilled in their motion of chopping herbs. "Did he ever mention changing it? After your argument?"

Antonio's jaw tightened. "He was angry, but *Nonno* wasn't cruel. Family is family, no matter what disagreements we had."

But Sophie caught the uncertainty in his voice, the way his eyes wouldn't quite meet Sofia's. Marco had been furious about Antonio's secret meetings with Vincenzo. Had the old man been serious about disinheriting his grandson?

Elena Costa arrived mid-morning with arms full of flowers from her garden and fierce determination written across her features. She embraced Sofia with the intensity of someone who understood loss, then immediately rolled up her sleeves to help with the food preparation.

"*Bastardi*," she muttered as she arranged white roses in a simple vase. "To call Marco's death an accident when anyone with eyes can see what really happened."

"Elena," Sofia warned quietly, glancing toward Antonio.

"No, I will not be quiet about this," Elena replied, her voice rising. "Marco died because he wouldn't sell to developers. Now watch—within a week, that *serpente* Vincenzo will come sniffing around with offers to 'help' the grieving family."

As if summoned by her words, the sound of expensive car tires on gravel announced a visitor. Through the window, Sophie watched a black Alfa Romeo, pull up to the house. Vincenzo Rossi stepped out, dressed in perfectly tailored mourning attire, his expression appropriately solemn.

"Speak of the devil," Elena hissed.

Vincenzo entered the kitchen with the careful demeanor of someone walking on sacred ground. He carried flowers—white lilies that must have cost more than most of the local families spent on food in a week—and his condolences were delivered with practiced sincerity.

"Sofia, my deepest sympathies," he said, taking her hands in his manicured ones. "Marco was a true gentleman, a man who loved this land more than life itself."

"*Grazie*, Vincenzo," Sofia replied stiffly.

He turned to Antonio with slightly more warmth. "And Antonio, please know that if there's anything you need during this difficult time—legal assistance, financial advice, anything at all—you have only to ask."

Elena made a sound that might have been a cough or might have been an expression of disgust. Vincenzo's smile never wavered, but his eyes hardened slightly as they fixed on her.

"*Signora* Costa, how lovely to see you. I trust you're well?"

"Well enough to see through false sympathy," Elena replied tartly.

The temperature in the room seemed to drop several degrees. Vincenzo's composure cracked just enough to show the calculation beneath his polished exterior.

"I'm sure grief affects us all differently," he said smoothly. "Marco's loss is devastating for the entire community. He was the last of the old guard, the final keeper of traditions that may not survive in this modern world."

The implication hung in the air like smoke from a funeral pyre. Traditional methods had died with Marco. Modern solutions would be needed now.

"The traditions will survive," Sofia said firmly. "We'll make sure of that."

"Of course," Vincenzo agreed. "Though it won't be easy. The expenses of maintaining traditional methods, the challenges of competing with industrial operations... these are burdens that fall heavily on grieving families."

Sophie watched this verbal chess match with growing anger. The man was using Marco's funeral as an opportunity to plant seeds of doubt about the family's ability to continue their operation. His timing was calculated and cruel.

Before she could voice her outrage, another car pulled into the drive. Sophie's heart sank as she recognized Ryan's rental sedan. Her ex-husband stepped out wearing an expensive dark suit and an expression of practiced sympathy that made her stomach turn.

"I hope I'm not intruding," Ryan said as he entered the kitchen. "I heard about Mr. De Luca's tragic accident and wanted to pay my respects."

Sophie stared at him, wondering how he'd heard about Marco's death so quickly. They'd spoken at dinner just two nights ago, and he'd mentioned knowing Marco only in passing. Now he was here, offering condolences like a close family friend.

"Ryan, what are you really doing here?" she asked directly.

Ryan's gaze flicked to Vincenzo, and something passed between them—a look of recognition that confirmed Sophie's growing suspicions.

Vincenzo gave the smallest nod—one Sophie might have missed if she hadn't been watching for it. Not greeting, but confirmation. Agreement.

"Actually," Ryan said, his tone shifting to something more businesslike, "I was hoping to speak with Antonio about some investment opportunities that might help the family during this transition."

The pieces clicked into place in Sophie's mind with sickening clarity. Ryan's mysterious business in Italy, his sudden appearance in Tuscany, his vague explanations about "reconnecting with suppliers"—he was working with Vincenzo.

"Investment opportunities?" Sofia's voice carried a dangerous edge. "What kind of investments?"

Vincenzo stepped forward smoothly. "Nothing that needs concern us today. This is a time for mourning, not business. Perhaps we should—"

"No," Antonio interrupted, his voice heavy with exhaustion. "If there are options that could help secure our future, I want to hear them."

Elena slammed down the vase she'd been arranging with enough force to rattle the kitchen table. "*Madonna mia!* Is there no respect left in this world? The man's body isn't even in the ground, and you vultures are already circling!"

Sofia's gaze sharpened. "You're not here to mourn. You're here to value the property. Like an appraiser in a suit."

"Elena's right," Sophie said, her anger finally breaking free. "This is disgraceful. Ryan, I want you to leave. Now."

Ryan's expression hardened. "Sophie, you don't understand the financial pressures this family is facing. Without help, they could lose everything Marco worked for."

"Help?" Sofia's voice rose to match her anger. "You call stealing our land 'help'?"

"No one's talking about stealing anything," Vincenzo said with practiced reasonableness. "We're talking about partnerships that could preserve the essential character of this operation while ensuring its financial viability."

"By turning it into a theme park for tourists," Elena spat.

The argument might have escalated further, but the arrival of Father Benedetto, the local priest, brought an abrupt end to the confrontation. The elderly cleric took in the scene with sharp eyes, his presence immediately commanding respect and restoring some semblance of appropriate behavior.

"*Buongiorno*," he said quietly. "I've come to discuss arrangements for Marco's funeral. Perhaps this is not the best time for business discussions?"

Vincenzo and Ryan took the hint, offering final condolences before making their exits. But not before Vincenzo pressed a business card into Antonio's hand.

"When you're ready to discuss the future," he said quietly. "Day or night."

After they left, the kitchen felt lighter but also more tense. Father Benedetto's presence was comforting, but his gentle questions about Marco's final days brought the reality of loss crashing back over the family.

"He was troubled these past weeks," Sofia admitted as they discussed the funeral arrangements. "More than usual. He kept talking about people watching the property, asking questions that made him uncomfortable."

"What kind of questions?" the priest asked gently.

"About the war years," Antonio said, surprising everyone. "I overheard him on the phone with the church records office in Florence, asking about documents from 1943. Something about property transfers and families who fled during the German occupation."

Father Benedetto's expression grew thoughtful. "The war years were difficult for many families. Records were lost, properties changed hands under duress. Perhaps Marco was trying to resolve old questions before..."

He didn't finish the sentence, but the implication hung in the air. Had Marco been trying to settle old accounts before his death? Or had his research into wartime records somehow led to his murder?

As the afternoon wore on and more neighbors arrived to pay their respects, Sophie found herself studying each visitor, wondering who might have wanted Marco dead. Paolo Bianchi came with genuine tears and a wreath of olive branches. Gabriella arrived with flowers and what seemed like sincere grief, though Sophie noticed how her eyes kept drifting to Antonio with an expression Sophie couldn't quite read—soft, but not warm. Like someone weighing options.

Elena stayed through the day, helping with food preparation and acting as Sofia's fierce protector against anyone who seemed to be taking advantage of the family's grief. When the mayor arrived with official condolences and carefully worded questions about the family's plans for the property, Elena intercepted him at the door.

"This is a house of mourning," she told him firmly. "Official business can wait until after the funeral."

As evening approached and the last of the visitors departed, Sophie found herself alone in the kitchen with

Sofia, who sat staring at an untouched cup of coffee with hollow eyes.

"Sofia," Sophie said gently, "there's something I need to ask you. Marco's journal—did he keep records of his concerns about the property? His suspicions about who might be threatening the family?"

Sofia looked up with eyes red from crying. "Why do you ask?"

"Because I think his death wasn't random. Someone killed him to protect secrets, and those secrets might be written down somewhere."

Sofia was quiet for a long moment, then stood and walked to an old wooden cabinet in the corner. She reached behind some cookbooks and withdrew a worn leather journal, its pages yellowed with age.

"*Nonno* asked me to give this to you if anything happened to him," she said, her voice barely above a whisper. "He said you had 'eyes that see truth' and that you might understand things the family was too close to recognize."

Sophie accepted the journal with trembling hands, feeling the weight of Marco's trust and the responsibility it carried. "When did he ask you to do this?"

"Two days ago, the morning after his argument with Antonio. He seemed... frightened. Not of dying, but of what might happen to the family's secrets if he wasn't here to protect them."

Sophie opened the journal carefully, seeing page after page filled with Marco's careful handwriting in a mixture of Italian and English. The entries went back decades, recording everything from weather patterns and olive yields to family events and business decisions.

But it was the recent entries that made her blood run cold. Marco's writing became increasingly agitated as he documented "strangers asking questions about wartime records," "surveyors on the property without permission," and "offers that seem designed to force a sale rather than purchase property."

The final entry, dated the morning of his death, was written in a shaky hand that suggested either great age or great fear:

They were in the grove again last night. Digging near the old stone. Looking for what Papa buried in 1943. If they find it, everything changes. The shame, the guilt, the secrets we've carried for eighty years—all of it will come out. Must speak with Sofia today, tell her where the real documents are hidden. Some truths are too dangerous to leave unprotected. But if I die before telling Sofia, the land will carry the truth —until someone brave enough is willing to listen

Sophie looked up to find Sofia watching her with desperate hope. "What does it say?"

"Marco knew someone was searching for something buried near the boundary stone. Something from 1943 that your family has been protecting ever since."

Sofia's face went pale. "The war years. *Nonno* never talked about them, said they were too painful to remember. But there were always whispers in the family—about choices that had to be made, about survival requiring compromise."

Before Sophie could ask more questions, the sound of footsteps on the stairs announced Antonio's return from his meeting with the lawyer. His face was grim as he entered the kitchen, carrying a folder of legal documents.

"How bad is it?" Sofia asked.

Antonio sank into a chair, suddenly looking older than his years. "Worse than we thought. The medical bills from *Nonno*'s treatments, the equipment repairs, the declining olive prices—we're in serious debt. Without a cash infusion soon, we might have to sell part of the property just to stay afloat."

"The disputed section?" Sophie asked.

"That would solve our immediate problems," Antonio admitted. "Twenty hectares that we're fighting over anyway, that costs us more in legal fees than it produces in revenue. Vincenzo's offering is enough to clear our debts and modernize our operation."

"At what cost?" Sofia demanded. "Once he has a foothold on our land, how long before he wants the rest?"

Antonio's phone buzzed with a text message. He glanced at it, and his expression grew even more troubled.

"What is it?" Sofia asked.

"Vincenzo. He wants to meet tonight to discuss 'time-sensitive opportunities.' He says there are other interested parties, and if we don't act soon, we might lose our chance to sell on favorable terms."

Sophie felt the pieces of the puzzle shifting in her mind. The pressure to sell, Marco's research into wartime records, the buried documents someone was searching for

—it all connected to the disputed land and whatever secrets lay hidden there.

"Antonio," she said carefully, "before you meet with Vincenzo, you should know what's in your grandfather's journal. Someone killed him to protect secrets that go back to the war. Whatever's buried on your property, it's worth committing murder to keep hidden."

Antonio stared at her, then at the journal in her hands. "You think *Nonno* was murdered? The police said—"

"The police saw what someone wanted them to see," Sophie interrupted. "But Marco knew he was in danger. His final journal entry mentions people digging near the boundary stone, looking for documents his father buried in 1943. Documents that could change everything."

As if summoned by their conversation, the sound of a car approaching made all three of them freeze. Through the window, they could see headlights cutting through the darkness, coming up the drive toward the house.

"Too early for Vincenzo," Antonio muttered, checking his watch.

The car pulled to a stop, and a figure emerged from the driver's seat. In the porch light, Sophie recognized Paolo Bianchi, but his posture was different—urgent, almost desperate.

He knocked on the kitchen door with sharp, insistent raps.

"Paolo?" Sofia called through the door. "What's wrong?"

"I need to speak with Antonio," Paolo called back. "About what happened to Marco. About the documents we've all been fighting over. It wasn't an accident. And if you don't act tonight, someone else will die before morning."

Sophie, Sofia, and Antonio exchanged glances. Outside, Paolo waited in the darkness, carrying secrets that might finally explain why Marco De Luca had died among his beloved olive trees.

The harvest of truth was about to begin.

———

*FROM SOPHIE'S SUBSTACK: **Farm-to-Table Adventures***

"Tonight I hold a dead man's journal, filled with sixty years of careful observations about weather, harvests, and human nature. Marco's final entries speak of watchers in the night and secrets buried —secrets that someone was willing to kill to protect. Tomorrow we bury him among the olive trees he loved. But first, we must uncover the truth he died defending..."

CHAPTER 7
THE JOURNAL OF SECRETS

PAOLO BIANCHI STOOD in the kitchen doorway like a man carrying the weight of generations on his shoulders. His usual composed demeanor had cracked, revealing something raw and desperate underneath. His clothes were muddy, his hands dirty, and there was a wild look in his eyes that made Sophie instinctively step back.

"Paolo," Sofia said carefully, "come in. Sit down. You look terrible."

He shook his head, remaining in the doorway as if afraid that crossing the threshold would make his words irreversible. Outside, a car door slammed—too far away to see, but close enough to make him flinch.

"I can't stay long. People are watching, people who would kill me if they knew what I'm about to tell you."

"Then tell us," Antonio said, his voice sharp with tension. "Who killed my grandfather?"

Paolo's gaze swept the room, taking in the mourning preparations, Marco's journal still open in Sophie's hands, the funeral clothes laid out for tomorrow. When he spoke, his voice carried the weight of a confession decades in the making.

"It wasn't supposed to happen like this. Marco wasn't supposed to die." He ran a hand through his graying hair, leaving streaks of dirt. "We had an understanding, he and I. A secret agreement that was meant to protect both our families."

"What kind of agreement?" Sofia demanded.

Paolo stepped into the kitchen, closing the door behind him and checking the windows as if expecting watchers to emerge from the darkness. "The boundary dispute—it was never really about the land. It was about what's buried underneath it."

Sophie felt her pulse quicken. Marco's journal had mentioned documents buried during the war, secrets that someone was willing to kill for. "What's buried there?"

"Documents that could destroy families, ruin reputations, maybe even send people to prison," Paolo said grimly. "My grandmother told me stories before she died. Stories about choices people made during the war, about survival requiring compromise with the Germans."

The kitchen fell silent except for the ticking of the old clock. Sophie could see understanding dawning in Sofia's eyes, the terrible realization of what Paolo was suggesting.

"You're talking about collaboration," Sofia whispered.

Paolo nodded miserably. "Some families helped the partisans, hid Jews, fought the occupation. Others... others did what they had to do to survive. Or what they thought they had to do. The line between collaboration and survival was thin, and not everyone stayed on the right side of it."

Antonio sat heavily in his chair, the implications washing over him. "You're saying our families—"

"Were involved in things that would be unforgivable if they came to light today," Paolo finished. "The documents buried near that boundary stone contain records of transactions, agreements, maybe even lists of names. People who were betrayed to save others. Jews who were hidden in some places and reported in others. Partisans who were protected or exposed depending on which choice seemed safer at the time."

Sophie thought about Marco's final journal entry, his reference to "shame, guilt, and secrets carried for eighty years." The old man had been protecting more than just property—he'd been guarding his family's wartime legacy.

"But that was eighty years ago," she said. "Why does it matter now?"

Paolo's laugh was bitter. "Because some of those families still live here. Some of the descendants of people who were betrayed or saved are your neighbors, your customers, your friends. And because there are people today who would use those secrets to destroy anyone who stands in their way."

"Vincenzo," Antonio breathed.

"Among others," Paolo confirmed. "He's been researching wartime records for months, trying to find leverage against families who won't sell to him. The threat of exposure, of having your family's darkest secrets dragged into the light—it's more effective than any amount of money."

Sofia stood abruptly, her chair scraping against the floor. "Are you saying Vincenzo killed *Nonno* to get access to these documents?"

"I'm saying Marco died because he was the last person who knew exactly where they were buried and what they contained," Paolo replied. "He's been protecting those secrets his entire life, just as my family has been trying to find proof of what happened to our relatives who disappeared during the war."

Sophie looked down at Marco's journal, understanding flooding through her. The old man hadn't just been protecting property or tradition—he'd been the guardian of secrets that could destroy lives if they fell into the wrong hands.

"Paolo," she said carefully, "you said you and Marco had an agreement. What kind of agreement?"

Paolo's shoulders slumped with exhaustion. "We were going to find the documents together. Quietly, privately. Marco would tell me where they were buried, and I would help him destroy the most damaging portions while preserving anything that might give my family closure about our lost relatives."

"But something went wrong," Antonio said.

"Marco got suspicious. He thought someone was following him, watching the property. In his final phone call to me, he said he'd changed his mind about trusting anyone, even me. He was going to move the documents to a new hiding place."

Sophie felt the pieces clicking together. "So when he went for his walk that morning—"

"He was planning to retrieve the documents and hide them somewhere else. But someone was waiting for him. Someone who couldn't risk letting him move evidence that could expose their own family's wartime secrets."

The kitchen fell silent as the implications sank in.

Marco had died protecting secrets that weren't even his own, killed by someone desperate to keep their family's collaboration hidden.

"Do you know who it was?" Sofia asked quietly.

Paolo shook his head. "I have suspicions, but no proof. What I do know is that the documents are still buried near that boundary stone, and whoever killed Marco will be back to look for them."

As if summoned by his words, the sound of car engines approaching made everyone freeze. Through the window, Sophie could see headlights—multiple sets, moving slowly up the drive toward the house.

"*Merda*," Paolo cursed, moving to peer out the window. "They followed me."

"Who followed you?" Antonio demanded.

Before Paolo could answer, the distinctive sound of Vincenzo's expensive sedan became audible, followed by another car Sophie didn't recognize. The vehicles stopped in the courtyard, their engines ticking in the sudden silence.

"Hide the journal," Paolo said urgently to Sophie. "Whatever happens, don't let them see it. And don't trust anyone—not even family. The secrets in those documents have been corrupting people for generations."

A knock echoed through the house—polite but insistent. Vincenzo's voice carried through the door, smooth and reasonable as always.

"Antonio? I know it's late, but we need to talk. There have been some developments that affect your family's situation."

Sofia looked panicked. "What do we do?"

"Act normal," Paolo whispered. "Pretend I was just here

to pay respects. And whatever you do, don't let them know about the journal."

Sophie quickly tucked Marco's journal inside her jacket, feeling the weight of eighty years of secrets pressing against her ribs. As Antonio went to answer the door, she caught Paolo's arm.

"Where exactly are the documents buried?" she whispered.

"Three meters north of the boundary stone, one meter down. But Sophie—if you go looking for them, you might not live to tell what you find."

The kitchen door opened, and Vincenzo entered with his usual polished smile, followed by a man Sophie didn't recognize—tall, thin, wearing expensive clothes that couldn't quite hide the calculating coldness in his eyes.

His tie was a shade too flashy, his handshake oddly limp. Like a man who studied charm but never quite learned how to wear it.

"I hope I'm not interrupting," Vincenzo said, though his presence suggested he didn't much care if he was. "Antonio, this is my associate, Dr. Matteo Sardelli. He specializes in historical research and document authentication."

Sophie felt her blood turn cold. A document specialist, arriving just hours after Paolo had revealed the existence of buried wartime records. The timing was too convenient to be coincidental.

"We understand this is a difficult time," Dr. Sardelli said, his voice carrying a faint accent that might have been Roman. "But there are urgent matters regarding your property that require immediate attention."

"What kind of matters?" Sofia asked suspiciously.

Vincenzo's smile never wavered. "It's come to our

attention that there may be historically significant artifacts on your property. Documents or records from the war years that could be of immense value to researchers and historians."

Paolo's face had gone pale, but he managed to keep his voice steady. "What kind of documents?"

"The kind that families sometimes buried to keep them safe during the German occupation," Dr. Sardelli replied smoothly. "Property records, family histories, business transactions. Items that could provide fascinating insights into how people survived during those difficult years."

Sophie watched this verbal chess match with growing dread. They knew about the buried documents, but they weren't sure exactly where they were or what they contained. That's why they needed access to the property —and why Marco had died when he'd tried to move them.

"We're prepared to offer a very generous fee for permission to conduct a limited archaeological survey," Vincenzo continued. "Just a small section of the disputed land, nothing that would interfere with your olive production."

"How generous?" Antonio asked, and Sophie heard the weakness in his voice. The financial pressures were real, and Vincenzo was exploiting them expertly.

"Enough to cover your family's debts and fund the modernization your grandfather always resisted," Vincenzo replied. "All for a few days of careful excavation in an area you're already fighting over."

Paolo stood abruptly. "I should go. This is family business, and I've intruded long enough."

But as he moved toward the door, Dr. Sardelli blocked his path with casual efficiency. "Actually, Signor Bianchi, your perspective would be valuable. Your family has also been researching wartime records, haven't you? Perhaps we could combine our efforts."

The threat was subtle but unmistakable. They knew Paolo had been searching for the same documents, and they weren't going to let him leave until they understood how much he knew.

"I don't know what you're talking about," Paolo said, but his voice lacked conviction.

"Come now," Dr. Sardelli replied smoothly. "We're all civilized people here. Surely we can work together for everyone's benefit."

Sophie realized with growing horror that she was witnessing more than just business negotiation—this was an interrogation. Paolo was trapped, the family was being manipulated, and she was holding a journal that might contain the very information these men were willing to kill for.

Her phone buzzed with a text message, and she glanced at it discreetly:

Unknown Number: The old man couldn't keep his secrets buried. Don't make the same mistake.

It was the same number that had threatened her after Marco's death. Someone in this room—or working with someone in this room—was Marco's killer.

As the conversation continued around her, Sophie began planning her escape. She needed to get Marco's journal to safety, needed to examine the buried documents before these men could destroy or manipulate them. Most importantly, she needed to find proof of who had killed Marco and why.

But first, she had to survive this encounter. The men who had murdered an eighty-three-year-old man to protect their secrets wouldn't hesitate to eliminate a nosy American food blogger.

The harvest of truth was about to become very dangerous indeed.

"Actually," she said, forcing her voice to remain steady, "I should probably head back to my room. It's been an emotional day, and I have an early flight tomorrow."

It was a lie, but it might give her a reason to leave before things escalated further.

Vincenzo's eyes sharpened with interest. "Leaving so soon, Miss Brooks? I thought you were here to document traditional olive oil production. Surely Marco's death hasn't changed your professional obligations?"

There was something in his tone that made Sophie's skin crawl—a suggestion that her departure might not be as simple as buying a plane ticket.

"My work here is finished," she replied carefully. "I have what I need for my article."

"But do you really?" Dr. Sardelli asked, moving closer to her. "I suspect you've learned more about this family's history than you bargained for. Perhaps you'd be interested in hearing the complete story before you leave?"

Sophie felt the journal pressing against her side like a hidden weapon. These men suspected she knew something, but they weren't sure what. Her best chance was to play dumb and get out of the house before they decided she was too dangerous to let go.

"I'm just a food blogger," she said with what she hoped was convincing innocence. "Family history isn't really my area of expertise."

Paolo caught her eye and gave an almost imperceptible nod, as if encouraging her to maintain the facade. But the strain of keeping secrets was written across his face, and Sophie worried he might crack under pressure.

"Of course," Vincenzo said smoothly. "Though I should mention—for your own safety—that there have been some dangerous individuals in the area lately. People looking for items that don't belong to them, people who might not hesitate to harm innocent tourists who stumble into situations they don't understand."

The threat was clear. Leave quietly, or face the same fate as Marco.

But Sophie had come too far to back down now. Somewhere in this web of wartime legacy and modern greed lay the truth about Marco's murder. She owed it to the old man—and to his family—to uncover it.

"I appreciate the warning," she said, moving toward the door. "I'll be very careful."

As she left the kitchen, she could feel eyes watching her every movement. The journal seemed to burn against her side, carrying information that men were willing to kill for.

She'd come here to write about olive oil. Now she was carrying evidence that might rewrite wartime history—and get her killed in the process.

Tomorrow would bring the planning of Marco's funeral and what was supposed to be a celebration of the olive harvest. But Sophie suspected it would also bring a confrontation that had been building for eighty years—a final reckoning between the living and the dead, between truth and the lies people told to survive.

In her room, she carefully hid Marco's journal beneath her mattress and began planning her next move. There were still a few hours before the funeral. Enough time to find the boundary stone again—alone.

She had until dawn to figure out how to expose Marco's killer without becoming the next victim.

---

*From Sophie's Substack: **Farm-to-Table Adventures***

"Tonight I learned that the most dangerous harvests aren't always about crops. Some families have been cultivating secrets for generations, tending them like poisonous plants that grow more toxic with time. Marco died protecting truths that could destroy lives if exposed. Now the question is: which lives, and whether the truth is worth the cost of revealing it..."

CHAPTER 8
DINNER & DECEPTIONS

SOPHIE BARELY SLEPT THAT NIGHT, Marco's journal hidden beneath her mattress like a dangerous secret. Every sound outside her window—the rustle of olive leaves, the distant bark of a dog, the settling of old wood—sent her heart racing with the possibility that someone was coming for the evidence she protected. When dawn finally crept through her shutters, she felt exhausted but grimly determined.

The morning brought a flurry of activity as the household prepared for Marco's funeral. Black-clad neighbors arrived with flowers and food, their voices hushed with respect for the dead and worry for the living. Sophie helped where she could, but her mind remained focused on the secrets buried beneath the ancient boundary stone and the men who were willing to kill to control them.

It was mid-morning when her phone buzzed with an unexpected message from Ryan:

> Ryan: I know last night was awkward, but I need to talk to you privately. There are things about my work here that I can't discuss in front of others. Meet me for lunch at Café Centrale in Montepulciano? It's important.

Sophie stared at the message, suspicion warring with curiosity. After witnessing Ryan's obvious connection to Vincenzo, she had no interest in his explanations or apologies. But if he was part of the conspiracy that had killed Marco, she needed to understand his role in it.

> Sophie: Fine. But this better be good. And it better be honest.

> Ryan: More honest than I've been about anything in years. You'll understand when we talk.

At noon, Sophie found herself walking through the cobblestone streets of Montepulciano toward Café Centrale, a small restaurant tucked into one of the town's medieval buildings. The funeral wasn't until evening, giving her time for this confrontation, but she felt guilty leaving Sofia to handle the preparations alone.

Ryan was already seated at a corner table when she arrived, his expression unusually serious. He'd traded his expensive suit for casual clothes, but he still looked out of place among the local diners with his obvious American prosperity.

"Thank you for coming," he said as she sat down, not attempting his usual charming smile. "I know you have every reason to distrust me."

"That's an understatement," Sophie replied coldly. "What are you really doing here, Ryan? And don't give me any more lies about investment opportunities."

Ryan was quiet for a moment, studying her face as if trying to decide how much truth she could handle. When he spoke, his voice carried a weariness she'd never heard before.

"I'm investigating Vincenzo Rossi for financial fraud," he said simply. "I work for a consortium of American restaurant owners who've been defrauded by his import operation. We're talking about millions of dollars in losses."

Sophie studied his face, trying to gauge how deep he was. If Vincenzo suspected him, Ryan could end up buried in the same soil as Marco.

Sophie blinked, not sure she'd heard correctly. "You're investigating him? But last night you seemed to be working with him."

"Deep cover," Ryan replied grimly. "I've been building a relationship with his organization for months, pretending to be a potential investor while gathering evidence of his schemes. The restaurants he claims to supply don't exist, the olive oil he imports is industrial-grade stuff relabeled as premium product, and the 'traditional family operations' he partners with are mostly figments of his imagination."

The revelation hit Sophie like a physical blow. Ryan—her lying, cheating ex-husband—was actually investigating the man she suspected of murder?

"Why didn't you tell me this before?" she demanded.

"Because I couldn't risk blowing my cover, and because..." He hesitated, then met her eyes directly.

"Because I was afraid you wouldn't trust me enough to help. Our marriage ended badly, Sophie. I know I lost the right to ask for your faith."

Sophie felt her worldview shifting uncomfortably. For days, she'd been certain that Ryan was part of the conspiracy against the De Luca family. Now he was claiming to be on the side of justice?

"Prove it," she said simply.

Ryan reached into his jacket and withdrew a small recording device, setting it on the table between them. "Three hours of conversations with Vincenzo about his plans for the De Luca property. Including some very interesting details about his research into wartime records and his willingness to use 'historical irregularities' to pressure families into selling."

Sophie stared at the device, her mind racing. "You recorded him talking about using wartime secrets as blackmail?"

"Among other things. He's been systematic about it—targeting families with questionable histories, offering to help them 'manage potential embarrassment' in exchange for property deals. It's extortion disguised as business."

Before Sophie could respond, the café door opened and Antonio entered, looking around nervously before spotting their table. He approached with hesitant steps, his face drawn with grief and stress.

"Sophie? I hope I'm not interrupting, but I got your message about meeting for lunch." He glanced uncertainly at Ryan. "Though I didn't expect..."

Sophie realized with growing unease that she hadn't sent Antonio any message. Someone had lured him here, using her name to ensure his presence.

"Antonio, I didn't—" she began. Her mouth went dry. Someone had lured him here under her name. A text she hadn't sent. That meant her phone was compromised—or someone had access to Antonio's too. She was interrupted by the arrival of Vincenzo Rossi and Dr. Sardelli, both wearing expressions of polite satisfaction as they approached the table.

"What a pleasant surprise," Vincenzo said smoothly, though his smile suggested this meeting was anything but accidental. "All the key players gathered in one place. How convenient. And Sophie—still here in Tuscany, when I thought you'd be on a plane home by now. Curious."

Sophie felt trapped, realizing she'd walked into some kind of setup. But whose setup? Had Ryan betrayed her, or was he as surprised by this development as she was?

"Vincenzo," Ryan said carefully, his tone neutral. "I wasn't expecting to see you here."

"Of course not," Vincenzo replied, settling into an empty chair without invitation. Dr. Sardelli remained standing, positioning himself where he could watch the restaurant's entrance. "But when opportunities arise to clarify misunderstandings, one must seize them."

Antonio looked confused and increasingly uncomfortable. "What misunderstandings?"

"The unfortunate confusion about your family's historical documents," Dr. Sardelli said smoothly. "It seems there have been some wild theories circulating about buried records and wartime secrets. We thought it best to address these fantasies before they damage anyone's reputation."

Sophie caught the subtle threat in his words. They knew she'd been talking to Paolo, knew she understood what was really at stake. This wasn't a chance encounter—

it was a confrontation designed to gauge how much their enemies knew and what they planned to do about it.

"I'm just here for lunch," she said carefully. "I don't know anything about historical documents."

"Of course not," Vincenzo agreed, but his eyes remained cold. "Though it's interesting how often your name comes up in conversations about the De Luca property. Marco seemed quite fond of you, quite trusting. Perhaps too trusting."

The reference to Marco's death sent a chill down Sophie's spine. Was Vincenzo admitting to murder, or simply making a threat?

"Marco was a wonderful man," Antonio said firmly. "His death was a terrible accident."

"Accidents happen so easily on farms," Dr. Sardelli observed. "Old men climbing ladders they shouldn't climb, trusting equipment that's past its prime. Such tragedies could be avoided with proper modernization."

Sophie felt Ryan tense beside her, his hand moving instinctively toward his jacket where she suspected he carried another recording device. This conversation was becoming evidence of intimidation, if not outright confession.

"Gentlemen," Ryan said, his voice taking on a harder edge, "I think you're making everyone uncomfortable. Perhaps we should discuss business matters privately."

"But this is business," Vincenzo replied, his mask of politeness slipping slightly. "The business of ensuring that sensitive historical information doesn't fall into the wrong hands. The business of protecting families from embarrassing revelations about their wartime activities."

Antonio's face went pale. "What wartime activities?"

"The kind that families prefer to forget," Dr. Sardelli said with fake sympathy. "Choices people made to survive, compromises with occupying forces, information shared to protect some relatives at the expense of others. The past is full of such uncomfortable truths."

Sophie watched Antonio's reaction carefully, seeing understanding dawn in his eyes. The De Luca family's wartime secrets weren't just abstract history—they were personal shame that could destroy the family's reputation if exposed.

"You're threatening us," Antonio said quietly.

"We're offering to help you," Vincenzo corrected smoothly. "Partner with us, allow us to manage the sensitive archaeological aspects of your property, and any unfortunate documents that might surface can be handled discretely. Everyone benefits."

"And if we refuse?" Antonio asked.

Vincenzo's smile became predatory. "Then we can't control what researchers might uncover, or how the media might interpret historical findings. Reputations built over generations can be destroyed overnight by the wrong kind of publicity."

The threat was crystal clear now. Submit to blackmail, or face exposure of wartime collaboration that would ruin the family name and likely destroy their business. Sophie realized she was watching the same pattern that had likely led to Marco's death—pressure that escalated until someone felt they had no choice but to eliminate the threat.

Her phone buzzed with a text message. She glanced at it discreetly and felt her blood run cold:

Unknown Number: Stop playing games. You have

something that belongs to us. Return it, or join the old man.

She looked up to find Dr. Sardelli watching her with calculating eyes, as if he could read her thoughts. The message hadn't come from him—his hands were visible on the table—but someone in his network was monitoring her communications.

"Is everything alright?" Ryan asked, noticing her expression.

"Fine," Sophie lied, but she saw him catch the tension in her voice.

Vincenzo stood, his movement causing Dr. Sardelli to straighten attentively. "Well, this has been illuminating. Antonio, I hope you'll consider our conversation carefully. The offer stands, but time is a factor. Historical research waits for no one."

"And Sophie," Dr. Sardelli added, his voice carrying unmistakable menace, "I hope you'll remember that some stories are better left untold. For everyone's safety."

After they left, the three remaining at the table sat in heavy silence. Sophie could feel both men studying her, trying to understand what had just happened and what role she played in it.

"Sophie," Ryan said quietly, "what aren't you telling me? Those men aren't just after property—they're after something specific. Something they think you have."

She looked at Antonio, seeing fear and confusion warring in his expression. He was caught between pressures he didn't fully understand, inheriting not just a vineyard but generations of dangerous secrets.

"They want Marco's journal," she said finally.

It was still hidden beneath her mattress at the farm-house—unless someone had already found it.

Ryan blinked. "What journal?"

Sophie made a decision that felt like stepping off a cliff. If she was going to survive this, she needed allies. Real ones.

"Your grandfather kept records of everything—including his suspicions about who was threatening your family and why. He also wrote about documents buried during the war, documents that certain people would kill to suppress."

Ryan leaned forward, his expression sharpening. "Documents that could be evidence of wartime collaboration?"

"Among other things," Sophie confirmed. "Marco died protecting secrets that go back eighty years. And now those men think I know where to find them."

Antonio's face crumpled as the implications hit him. "You're saying *Nonno* was murdered? That someone killed him for documents hidden since the war?"

"I'm saying your grandfather was a guardian of truths that powerful people want to stay buried," Sophie replied gently. "And now that guardianship has passed to you."

As they sat in the café, surrounded by the normal sounds of lunch conversation and clinking dishes, Sophie felt the weight of Marco's trust settling more heavily on her shoulders. She had evidence of conspiracy and murder, but she also had a target painted on her back by people who had already demonstrated their willingness to kill.

Tomorrow was the harvest festival, when the entire community would gather to celebrate the olive harvest. It would be the perfect opportunity to expose the truth—or the perfect opportunity for her enemies to silence her permanently.

But first, she had to survive Marco's funeral. And she had to decide whether she could trust Ryan enough to let him help her, or whether his investigation into Vincenzo was just another elaborate deception.

The harvest of secrets was about to reach its climax, and Sophie was no longer sure who among the players could be trusted with the truth.

---

*FROM SOPHIE'S SUBSTACK: **Farm-to-Table Adventures***

"Today I learned that the most dangerous recipes are sometimes the ones passed down through generations—family secrets mixed with wartime shame, seasoned with decades of silence, and served with threats that taste like poison. Some ingredients are too toxic to bring into the light, but leaving them buried only makes them more dangerous..."

CHAPTER 9
BURIED EVIDENCE

THE AFTERNOON SUN slanted through the windows of Marco's study as Sophie and Sofia sat surrounded by the detritus of a life spent in careful record-keeping. Account books dating back decades, correspondence with suppliers, receipts for equipment repairs---every aspect of the vineyard's operation had been meticulously documented by Marco's patient hand.

But it was what they weren't finding that troubled Sophie most.

"There should be soil analysis reports," Sofia said, flipping through another folder with growing frustration. "Every few years, *Nonno* would have the disputed land tested. He was obsessive about understanding what made those twenty hectares so special."

Sophie looked up from the letter she'd been reading---a routine inquiry from a potential customer about their organic certification. "When was the last testing done?"

"In the spring. He mentioned sending samples to the laboratory in Florence, said he wanted to document the soil quality before..." Sofia's voice trailed off as the implication hit her. "Before he died."

The words hung heavy in the air between them. Marco had been preparing for something, documenting evidence as if he'd known time was running out.

"The results should be here somewhere," Sophie said, scanning the neat stacks of papers on Marco's desk. "He was too organized to lose something that important."

They worked in methodical silence, checking every folder, every drawer, every file. But the soil analysis reports were nowhere to be found. What they did find, however, painted a picture of a man under increasing pressure---invoices for legal fees related to the boundary dispute, correspondence with surveyors, and a series of increasingly aggressive letters from Vincenzo's legal team.

It was Sofia who discovered the hidden compartment.

"Mamma mia," she breathed, running her fingers along the inside edge of Marco's massive desk drawer. "There's something here."

Sophie leaned closer as Sofia pressed against what appeared to be solid wood. With a soft click, a thin panel slid aside, revealing a space barely large enough to hold a few documents.

Inside was a manila envelope marked "PRIVATE - S. ONLY" in Marco's careful handwriting.

Sofia's hands trembled as she opened it. "S for Sofia?" she whispered.

"Or Sophie," Sophie replied quietly. "He asked you to give me his journal if anything happened to him. Maybe this was meant for me too."

The envelope contained three documents: a copy of Marco's will dated just one week before his death, a letter addressed to Sofia, and a laboratory report stamped with the seal of the University of Florence Geological Department.

Sofia read the letter first, her face growing pale as she absorbed her grandfather's words. When she finished, she looked up at Sophie with eyes bright with unshed tears.

"He changed his will," she said simply. "Antonio isn't the sole heir anymore. The disputed twenty hectares---they come to me directly, with specific instructions that they're never to be sold or developed."

Sophie felt a chill run down her spine. "When did he make this change?"

"The day after his confrontation with Antonio about Vincenzo. The same day he asked me to give you his journal." Sofia's voice grew stronger as understanding dawned. "He knew, Sophie. He knew someone was going to try to kill him."

Sophie picked up the soil analysis report, her hands steady despite the magnitude of what they were uncovering. The technical language was dense, full of geological terms she didn't fully understand, but the summary was clear enough:

Soil samples from the disputed boundary area show unusually high concentrations of rare earth minerals, particularly neodymium and europium. These concentrations suggest potential commercial mining opportunities that would require further geological surveys to fully assess.

"My God," Sophie breathed. "This isn't about olives. It's about minerals---rare, valuable, strategic ones."

Sofia looked over her shoulder at the report. "What does it mean?"

"They're used in electronics, renewable energy technology, electric car batteries---basically everything that drives the modern economy." Sophie's mind raced through the implications. "If there are significant deposits under that land..."

"It would be worth millions," Sofia finished, understanding flooding her features. "Far more than any olive grove."

"And it would explain why Vincenzo is so determined to get access to that specific section of your property. The letters might give him legal leverage, but that's only part of it. He's not just building a resort—he's positioning himself to exploit what lies beneath the soil too. Minerals that could make him incredibly wealthy."

Sophie's phone buzzed with a message from Nate, and she felt a wash of relief at seeing his name.

> Nate: Hey, just checking in. How are you holding up after everything that's happened? Been thinking about you.

She didn't know what scared her more---how comforting it felt to hear from him, or how much she wanted him here. She typed back quickly:

> Sophie: Discovered something huge about why Marco was killed. Not just about wartime secrets---there are valuable minerals on the disputed land. Vincenzo's been planning this for months.

Nate: That sounds incredibly dangerous, Sophie. Are you somewhere safe?

Sophie: At the farmhouse with Sofia. We found evidence that Marco knew he was in danger---he changed his will days before he died.

Nate: I'm worried about you. These people have already killed once. Promise me you'll be careful.

Sophie: I promise. But I can't stop now. Marco trusted me with this, and his family deserves justice.

Nate: Then let me help. I can be on a plane tonight if you need me.

Sophie felt her heart warm at his offer, even as she recognized the danger of involving him.

Sophie: I may take you up on that. Let me see how tonight goes first.

As she tucked her phone away, Sofia was studying the geological report with growing excitement and anger.

"Look at this," Sofia said, pointing to a section of the technical analysis. "The samples were taken from multiple locations across the disputed area. The highest concentrations are right near the ancient boundary stone---exactly where Marco said people were digging at night."

"Someone else knew about the mineral deposits," Sophie realized. "That's why they were searching near the boundary stone. They weren't just looking for wartime documents---they were looking for geological surveys that would prove the land's value."

Sofia stood abruptly, pacing to the window that looked

out over the disputed grove. "This changes everything. If we can prove that Vincenzo knew about the minerals when he made his offers to buy the land..."

"It's fraud," Sophie finished. "He was offering to pay for agricultural land while knowing it was worth exponentially more for mining rights."

"But how do we prove he knew?" Sofia turned back to Sophie, determination replacing the grief that had haunted her features for days. "The soil report is dated just two months ago. Marco only just discovered this himself."

Sophie thought about the timing, about Vincenzo's increasingly aggressive pursuit of the property, about the sophisticated team he'd assembled to research "historical documents."

"I think someone tipped him off," she said slowly. "Someone with access to the laboratory, or someone who knew Marco was having the soil tested. That's why the pressure on your family intensified so suddenly."

"But who would have known?"

Before Sophie could answer, the sound of car tires on gravel announced another visitor. Through the window, they could see Paolo Bianchi climbing out of his truck, but his usual composed demeanor was replaced by obvious agitation. He moved quickly toward the house, glancing over his shoulder as if he expected to be followed.

Sophie felt her chest tighten. She'd barely begun to process last night's revelations—and now Paolo was back, with more truth than she was ready to hear.

"Paolo looks upset," Sofia observed.

Sophie felt her pulse quicken. After last night's revelations about wartime secrets and buried documents, Paolo's arrival could mean several things---none of them good.

They met him at the kitchen door, and Sophie was shocked by his appearance. His clothes were disheveled, his hands dirty, and there was a wild look in his eyes that suggested a man pushed beyond his limits.

"We need to talk," he said without preamble. "All of us. There are things about the boundary dispute you don't understand, things that go deeper than family feuds or wartime secrets."

"Come in," Sofia said, though Sophie caught the wariness in her voice. "Sit down. You look terrible."

Paolo shook his head, remaining standing by the door. "I can't stay long. They're watching my property, monitoring my calls. But you need to know the truth before tonight."

"What truth?" Sophie asked.

Paolo's gaze shifted between them, as if trying to decide how much to reveal. "The mineral deposits. Marco wasn't the first to discover them."

Sophie felt the pieces clicking together with sickening clarity. "You knew. You've known all along."

"My family commissioned geological surveys twenty years ago, when we were still trying to prove our claim to the disputed land. We thought if we could demonstrate that the soil was different, more valuable, it would support our legal case." Paolo's voice was heavy with regret. "We never expected to find what we found."

"Rare earth minerals," Sofia said quietly.

Paolo nodded. "A deposit significant enough to change the entire valley's economy. But the surveys were conducted quietly, privately. We kept the results secret while we figured out how to proceed."

"And then?" Sophie prompted.

"And then Vincenzo Rossi contacted us. Someone had leaked information about our surveys---we never found out who. He offered to help us establish a legal claim to the land in exchange for mining rights." Paolo's expression darkened. "We were naive enough to believe him."

Sofia stared at him in disbelief. "You've been working with Vincenzo? All these years of boundary disputes, and you were working with him?"

"Not all of us," Paolo said quickly. "I was against the partnership from the beginning. But my cousin Andrea, who handles our legal affairs, convinced the family that it was our best chance to finally win the land claim."

Sophie's mind raced through the implications. "So Vincenzo has known about the mineral deposits for twenty years. He's been playing a very long game."

"Longer than you realize," Paolo replied grimly. "The wartime documents we've all been fighting over? They don't just contain records of collaboration or betrayal. They contain the original geological surveys from the 1940s, when the Fascist government was mapping Italy's natural resources for the war effort."

The revelation hit Sophie like a physical blow. "The documents buried near the boundary stone aren't just about family shame. They're about mineral wealth that's been hidden for eighty years."

"Exactly. And Marco figured it out. The recent soil testing wasn't random---he'd found references to the wartime surveys in his father's papers and wanted to verify if the minerals were still there."

Sofia sank into a chair, overwhelmed by the scope of the conspiracy. "So everyone has been lying. Vincenzo, you, even Nonno in the end."

"Marco wasn't lying," Paolo said firmly. "He was protecting your family from knowledge that could get you killed. When he realized that Vincenzo would stop at nothing to get those mineral rights, he knew he had to act."

"That's why he changed his will," Sophie realized. "To make sure the disputed land would never fall into the wrong hands."

Paolo nodded. "But changing his will wasn't enough. Marco had contacted authorities in Rome, was preparing to expose the entire conspiracy. Someone couldn't let that happen."

"Someone killed him to keep the truth buried," Sofia said, her voice barely above a whisper.

"They've already killed once. Do you think they'll hesitate again?" Paolo said, looking directly at Sophie. "The journal, the soil reports, maybe even the location of the buried wartime documents. They won't stop hunting until they silence you too."

As if summoned by his words, the distant sound of multiple car engines echoed across the valley. Through the window, Sophie could see dust clouds rising from the access road---several vehicles heading toward the farmhouse.

"They followed me," Paolo said, his face going white. "I led them right to you."

Sophie grabbed the envelope containing Marco's documents, her mind racing through their options. "Is there another way out of here?"

Sofia nodded, moving toward the back door. "Through the olive grove. There's an old path that leads to the main road."

But as they reached the door, the sound of footsteps on

gravel told them they were too late. Voices carried across the courtyard---Vincenzo's smooth tones mixed with others Sophie didn't recognize. Men with authority in their voices, men who sounded very much like they weren't planning to take no for an answer.

"Hide the documents," Paolo urged. "Whatever happens, don't let them get Marco's evidence."

Sophie looked around desperately, then made a decision. She moved to the kitchen fireplace, where Sofia's grandmother's old bread oven was built into the stone. Working quickly, she wrapped the envelope in a kitchen towel and shoved it behind the cool stone. If they didn't survive the night, the truth would be waiting in the hearth.

"If something happens to us," she said to Sofia, "the evidence is there. Make sure the right people find it."

A sharp knock echoed through the house, followed by Vincenzo's voice calling out in false friendliness.

"Antonio? Sofia? We've come to discuss the generous offer we made yesterday. I hope we can reach an understanding."

Sophie, Sofia, and Paolo looked at each other, each understanding that their lives had just changed irrevocably. The evidence they'd uncovered could expose a conspiracy decades in the making, but only if they survived long enough to share it.

The harvest of truth was about to face its most dangerous test.

"Remember," Paolo whispered as the knocking grew more insistent, "whatever they say, whatever they promise, they've already killed once to protect their secret. Don't trust anything."

As Sofia moved toward the front door, Sophie felt the

weight of Marco's trust settling on her shoulders one final time. The old man had died protecting his family's land and Italy's mineral wealth from those who would exploit both.

Now it was up to her to finish what he'd started.

---

*FROM SOPHIE'S SUBSTACK: **Farm-to-Table Adventures***

"Today I learned that some harvests are more valuable than anyone imagines. Beneath the olive groves of Tuscany lie treasures that men will kill for---not gold or silver, but the rare elements that power our modern world. Marco died protecting more than tradition. He died protecting Italy's future from those who would sell it to the highest bidder..."

CHAPTER 10
FESTIVAL AND FRICTION

THE CONFRONTATION at the farmhouse had been a masterclass in intimidation disguised as concern. Vincenzo and his associates—including two men Sophie didn't recognize who carried themselves like security personnel —had spent an hour probing for information about Marco's "research" while making thinly veiled threats about the dangers of "misunderstanding historical documents."

Paolo had played his part perfectly, maintaining that his visit was purely social while Vincenzo's men searched the public areas of the house for any evidence of the soil reports or wartime documents. They'd found nothing, thanks to Sophie's quick thinking with the bread oven, but their frustration was palpable when they finally left.

Now, twenty-four hours later, the village of Montepulciano was transforming itself for the annual olive harvest festival. Despite the shadow of Marco's death, the celebration would go on—a tribute to the old man's dedication to tradition, Sofia had declared, and a defiant statement that the community wouldn't be cowed by outside pressures.

Sophie stood in the main piazza, watching workers string lights between medieval buildings and set up stalls for the food vendors. The festival was both a celebration and a showcase—an opportunity for local producers to display their finest oils, for restaurants to offer special menus, and for families like the De Lucas to demonstrate the traditional methods that made Tuscan olive oil legendary.

"It's beautiful," she murmured to Sofia, who was directing the setup of their family's demonstration area. Despite everything, Sofia had insisted on participating, determined to honor her grandfather's memory by showing the world what he'd fought to preserve.

"*Nonno* would have loved this," Sofia replied, arranging bottles of their oil in a display that caught the afternoon light like liquid gold. "He always said the festival was when the community came together to remember why our work matters."

Sophie's phone buzzed with another message from Nate:

Nate: Just landed in Rome. Should be in Montepulciano by tonight. Are you sure you don't want me to come straight to the festival?

SHE TYPED BACK:

Sophie: Too public, too many people watching. Meet me at the farmhouse after midnight. There's something I need to show you.

Nate: Sophie, you're scaring me. What's really going on?

Sophie: I found evidence that could expose Marco's killer, but it's bigger than just murder. There's a conspiracy involving mineral rights that goes back decades.

Nate: Jesus. Okay, I'll stay away from the festival. But if you're in danger—

Sophie: I'll be careful. Having you nearby makes me feel safer already.

As she put her phone away, Sophie noticed Paolo approaching through the crowd. He moved carefully, obviously checking to make sure he wasn't being followed, and his face carried the strain of a man balancing on a knife's edge.

"Any word from your cousin Andrea?" Sofia asked quietly as Paolo reached their stall.

Paolo's expression darkened. "He's not answering my calls. I think Vincenzo has convinced him that silence is safer than honesty."

"Or Vincenzo has made sure he can't talk," Sophie said grimly.

The implications hung in the air between them. If Paolo's cousin—the one family member who'd been actively working with Vincenzo—had been silenced, it suggested the conspiracy was entering its final, most dangerous phase.

"There's something else," Paolo said, lowering his voice as a group of tourists passed nearby. "I've been asking discrete questions about the laboratory that processed

Marco's soil samples. The director received a very generous research grant from a private foundation last month—a foundation that traces back to shell companies owned by Vincenzo's organization."

Sophie felt her stomach clench. "He bought the results?"

"Or bought access to them. Someone at the lab made sure Vincenzo knew about the mineral deposits as soon as Marco's tests were complete. That's why the pressure on your family became so intense in the past few weeks."

Sofia's hands tightened on the bottle she was holding. "So *Nonno* walked into a trap. The moment he submitted those soil samples, he signed his own death warrant."

"Marco was smart enough to realize that," Paolo said. "That's why he changed his will and hid the documents. He knew someone would come for him."

Their conversation was interrupted by the arrival of Vincenzo himself, moving through the festival crowd with the confident air of a man who owned everything he surveyed. He was dressed casually but expensively, playing the role of a local businessman supporting community traditions while his eyes catalogued every detail of the festivities.

"Sofia, Paolo," he said warmly as he approached their stall. "What a beautiful display. Marco would be so proud to see his legacy honored this way."

Sophie watched Sofia's face carefully, seeing the effort it took for her to maintain polite composure. "Thank you, Vincenzo. We felt it was important to continue the demonstration despite our loss."

"Of course, of course. Tradition must continue." Vincenzo picked up one of the bottles, examining the label with apparent interest. "Though I can't help but wonder how sustainable these methods really are in the modern world. The costs, the labor intensity, the uncertainty of relying on weather and soil conditions..."

"Some things are worth preserving regardless of cost," Paolo said firmly.

Vincenzo's smile never wavered, but his eyes sharpened. "Ah, Paolo. I was hoping to see you here. Perhaps we could have a private conversation later? I believe there are some misunderstandings that need to be resolved."

"What kind of misunderstandings?" Sophie asked, stepping closer to Paolo in a gesture of support.

"Business matters that don't concern outsiders," Vincenzo replied smoothly, but there was a warning in his tone. "Though I should mention, Miss Brooks, that I've been told you're planning to leave soon. I hope your stay in Tuscany has been... educational."

The threat was subtle but unmistakable. Sophie met his gaze steadily. "Very educational. I've learned so much about how people here value their land and traditions."

"Indeed. Though sometimes outsiders misunderstand the complexities of local issues. It would be unfortunate if your writings gave readers the wrong impression about our community."

Before Sophie could respond, a commotion near the center of the piazza drew everyone's attention. Two men were arguing loudly in rapid Italian, their voices rising above the festival noise. Sophie recognized one of them as Elena's cousin—the olive producer whose oil she'd tasted at the market.

"That's strange," Sofia murmured. "Roberto never makes a scene in public."

They moved closer to see what was happening, and Sophie caught fragments of the heated exchange. Roberto was gesturing angrily toward a man she didn't recognize —middle-aged, well-dressed, carrying himself with the authority of someone accustomed to being obeyed.

"He's refusing to sell his oil to the festival organizers," Sofia translated quietly. "Says he's already committed his entire harvest to a private buyer."

Paolo's face went pale. "That's impossible. Roberto's been selling to the festival for twenty years. It's one of his biggest income sources."

The argument continued, drawing more onlookers, until Elena herself appeared and began speaking firmly to both men. Within minutes, she'd managed to separate them, but not before Sophie caught sight of something that made her blood run cold.

The well-dressed stranger was carrying a briefcase with the logo of Vincenzo's development company.

"He's buying up the local oil production," Sophie realized. "Not just land—he's cornering the entire market."

Vincenzo, who had been watching the confrontation with apparent amusement, turned back to their group. "Business disputes are so unfortunate at community celebrations. But sometimes change is necessary for progress."

"What kind of change?" Sofia demanded.

"The kind that ensures this region's products reach their full market potential," Vincenzo replied. "Small, family operations like yours produce excellent oil, but they lack the distribution networks and marketing expertise to compete globally. Partnership with larger organizations could benefit everyone."

"Partnership or takeover?" Paolo asked bluntly.

Vincenzo's mask slipped slightly, revealing the calculation beneath his polished exterior. "That depends entirely on how reasonable people choose to be."

The conversation was interrupted by the arrival of Dr. Sardelli and another man Sophie didn't recognize—younger, intense, carrying himself like someone used to getting his way through intimidation rather than charm.

"Ah, Dr. Sardelli," Vincenzo said warmly. "Perfect timing. I was just discussing the importance of preserving local traditions with our friends here."

Dr. Sardelli nodded politely, but his attention was focused on Sophie. "Miss Brooks, I trust you're enjoying the festival? Such a shame that your visit has been overshadowed by recent tragedies."

"Tragedies have a way of revealing truth," Sophie replied carefully.

"Indeed they do. Though sometimes the truth is more complex than it first appears." Dr. Sardelli moved closer, lowering his voice. "I understand you've been doing research into local history. I hope you've found our archives... complete."

The implication was clear—they knew she'd been searching for documents, and they wanted her to know that any evidence had been controlled or eliminated.

But Sophie had one advantage they didn't know about: Marco's hidden documents were still safely concealed in the bread oven, along with the soil analysis that proved the mineral deposits' existence.

"History has a way of preserving itself," she said. "Even when people try to bury it."

Dr. Sardelli's eyes hardened. "Some things are better left buried, Miss Brooks. For everyone's safety."

The younger man stepped forward, and Sophie caught sight of a small bulge under his jacket that suggested he was armed. "Perhaps the lady would enjoy seeing more of the festival," he said in accented English. "There are many interesting... exhibits."

Paolo moved protectively between Sophie and the stranger. "She's perfectly safe with us."

"Of course," Vincenzo said smoothly. "Though festivals can be crowded, chaotic places. Accidents happen so easily in crowds."

Sofia grabbed Sophie's arm, her grip tight with fear. "We should check on our demonstration," she said quickly. "Make sure everything is properly set up."

They began to move away from Vincenzo's group, but the younger man shadowed them, maintaining a casual distance while keeping them in sight. Sophie realized with growing alarm that they were being herded, subtly guided away from the main festival crowds toward a quieter area of the piazza.

"They're isolating us," she whispered to Paolo.

"I know. When I give the signal, run toward the church. There are too many people there for them to try anything public."

But before Paolo could create a distraction, Elena appeared from the crowd like an avenging angel, her face flushed with anger and determination.

"Vincenzo!" she called out loudly enough to attract attention from nearby festival-goers. "I need to speak with you about your people harassing my suppliers!"

Her arrival created exactly the kind of public scene that Vincenzo's men couldn't afford. Within moments, curious onlookers had gathered, drawn by Elena's obvious agitation and the promise of festival drama.

"There's been a misunderstanding," Vincenzo said, his voice carrying the practiced calm of someone used to defusing situations.

"No misunderstanding!" Elena shot back. "Your buyers are pressuring producers to break their commitments to the festival. This is supposed to be a celebration of community, not a business takeover!"

The crowd murmured in agreement, and Sophie saw several faces she recognized from the market—local producers and vendors who were clearly sympathetic to Elena's position.

Taking advantage of the distraction, Paolo guided Sophie and Sofia back toward the main festival area, where the crush of tourists and locals provided safety in numbers.

"That was close," Sofia breathed when they reached the relative security of the crowded piazza center.

"Too close," Sophie agreed. "They're getting desperate."

Her phone buzzed with another message, this one from an unknown number:

Unknown: The festival ends at midnight. So does your time in Tuscany. Leave tonight, or you won't leave at all.

Sophie showed the message to Paolo and Sofia, watching their faces go pale as they absorbed the final nature of the threat.

"That's it," Paolo said firmly. "We're calling the Carabinieri. This has gone too far."

"And tell them what?" Sophie asked. "That we suspect murder based on soil samples and an old man's journal?

They ruled Marco's death an accident. They won't reopen the case without concrete proof."

"Then we get proof," Sofia said, her voice carrying a determination that reminded Sophie powerfully of her grandfather. "Tonight, after the festival, we go to the boundary stone. We find those wartime documents and the geological surveys. We expose everything."

Paolo looked alarmed. "That's exactly what they're expecting us to do. It's suicide."

"Maybe," Sophie said slowly. "Or maybe it's the only way to end this. They can't kill all of us in front of witnesses, and once the truth is public..."

Her phone rang, interrupting her thoughts. Nate's name appeared on the screen, and she answered quickly.

"Sophie, thank God," his voice was tight with concern. "I've been following coverage of the festival online, and I don't like what I'm seeing. There are too many men in expensive suits who look like they're hunting rather than celebrating."

"You're not wrong," Sophie replied. "Things are coming to a head tonight. Can you meet us at the farmhouse after the festival ends?"

"I'll be there soon. But Sophie—if this is as dangerous as it sounds, maybe it's time to call in professional help."

"We're past that point," Sophie said, looking around at the festival crowds and realizing how many people could be caught in the crossfire if this escalated further. "I'll explain everything when I see you."

As the afternoon wore on and the festival reached its peak, Sophie found herself studying faces in the crowd, trying to distinguish between genuine celebrants and Vincenzo's watchers. The atmosphere was festive on the surface, but underneath she could feel the tension building like pressure in a wine barrel.

The traditional pressing demonstration was scheduled for sunset—Sofia's tribute to Marco's memory and their family's dedication to preserving ancient methods. But Sophie suspected it would become something else entirely: the final confrontation in a battle that had been brewing for generations.

As the sun bled into the Tuscan hills, Sophie braced herself. Tonight, tradition would meet reckoning. And someone would not leave Montepulciano alive.

---

*From Sophie's Substack: **Farm-to-Table Adventures***

"Tonight, the olive harvest festival celebrates traditions that have sustained this community for centuries. But some harvests are more dangerous than others. As the sun sets over Tuscany, I'm preparing for a different kind of pressing—one that will extract truth from secrets buried too long in Italian soil. Some traditions are worth fighting for. Others are worth dying to protect..."

CHAPTER 11
WHAT THE SOIL REVEALS

THEY MET at the farmhouse after the festival, slipping into the kitchen once the last of the neighbors had drifted home. The space was quiet now, the long table littered with empty platters and wineglasses, a few candles burning low. Sophie set Marco's journal on the scarred wood between them, its leather cover looking more fragile than the secrets it held.

Nate rubbed the back of his neck, hesitation flickering across his face. "I'll be honest, Soph—part of me wondered if I was crazy for flying out here. Back in Sonoma, I kept telling myself not to get pulled into your mysteries. But then your messages came, and... well." He gave a small shrug. "Here I am."

Nate leaned forward, eyes intent. "Walk me through it. All of it."

So she did—how Marco had kept decades of records, the hints about wartime documents buried near the boundary stone, and the threats that had already turned deadly. As she spoke, Nate's jaw tightened, his hand clenching around his coffee cup.

"You're telling me," he said finally, voice low, "that whoever killed Marco is still out there, watching you, and willing to kill again to keep this buried?"

Sophie nodded, her throat dry. "I can't prove it yet, but every instinct I have says yes."

For a moment, the only sound was the faint crackle of a candlewick. Then Nate reached across the table, covering her hand with his. "Then we don't face it alone. Not anymore."

Warmth spread through her chest at his steady grip. She hadn't realized until now just how much she'd been carrying alone.

"Be careful what you're volunteering for," she whispered, managing a wry smile.

"I'm serious, Soph. I've seen enough to know this isn't just a family feud. You've stumbled onto something bigger, and it scares the hell out of me."

His thumb brushed the back of her hand, grounding her. She wanted to believe him—to let herself lean into the safety he offered. But she also knew what happened to people who got too close.

"Then we get through it one step at a time," she said. "Tomorrow, I'll keep digging. Tonight, we sleep."

He searched her face for a long moment, then nodded reluctantly. "Tomorrow."

Only when exhaustion made further planning impossible did they part for the night.

THE MORNING after the festival arrived gray and subdued, matching the weight that had settled over the De Luca farmhouse. Sophie woke to find her room had been searched—not ransacked, but carefully rifled through by someone who knew how to look without leaving obvious traces. Her clothes had been moved slightly, her camera bag unzipped and rezipped, her laptop shifted just enough to know it had been examined.

Marco's journal remained safely hidden beneath her mattress, but the message was clear: they were being watched, their every move catalogued by people who had no qualms about violating the sanctuary of grief.

Downstairs, she found Sofia in the kitchen, staring at an envelope that had been slipped under the door during the night. The return address showed the University of Florence Geological Department.

"The new soil tests," Sofia said without looking up. "*Nonno* ordered them just days before he died. I'd forgotten all about them with everything that's happened."

Sophie felt her pulse quicken. After Paolo's revelations about mineral deposits and Vincenzo's decades-long conspiracy, these results could be the proof they needed—or the final nail in their coffin if the wrong people got hold of them.

"Have you opened it?" she asked carefully.

Sofia shook her head. "I was waiting for Antonio. This affects his inheritance as much as mine."

As if summoned by his name, Antonio appeared in the doorway, looking haggard after the festival's tensions. His face was drawn with exhaustion, but his eyes sharpened when he saw the envelope in Sofia's hands.

"The geological survey," he said heavily. "I wondered when those would arrive."

Sophie watched him carefully, noting the way his gaze flicked to the envelope and then away, as if he was afraid of what it might contain. "Did Marco tell you what he expected to find?"

"He mentioned wanting to document the soil composition before any development decisions were made," Antonio replied. "He said if we were going to fight for the land, we needed to know exactly what we were fighting for."

Sofia carefully opened the envelope, her hands trembling slightly. Inside were several pages of technical analysis, charts showing mineral compositions, and a summary written in the dry language of scientific reporting. She scanned the first page, her eyes widening as she absorbed the information.

"*Madonna mia*," she breathed. "Sophie, look at this."

Sophie leaned over Sofia's shoulder, reading the summary that would change everything:

Soil samples from the disputed boundary area show unusually high concentrations of rare earth elements, particularly neodymium, europium, and terbium. These concentrations, found at depths of 1.5 to 3 meters below surface level, suggest potential commercial mining opportunities. Further geological survey recommended to assess full extent of deposits.

The kitchen fell silent except for the ticking of the old clock. Sophie felt her mind racing through the implications —the real reason for Vincenzo's aggressive pursuit of the property, the timing of Marco's death just as he'd ordered these tests, the desperate search for wartime documents that might complicate mining rights.

"This isn't about olive groves," Antonio said quietly, sinking into a chair. "It never was."

Sophie pushed Marco's journal toward him, tapping the margins. "These aren't just notes—he was tracking soil tests, shipments, and names. Vincenzo already has scientists on his payroll. He knows exactly what's buried here."

Sofia's face paled. "So it's not speculation anymore. He has proof. And if he controls that land, he controls the future of this valley."

Antonio picked up the report, studying the technical details with growing agitation. "Look at these concentration levels. This isn't just valuable—it's a game-changer for the entire region."

Sophie thought about Vincenzo's sophisticated operation, his team of researchers, his patient decades-long strategy. "He's known about this for a long time. The question is how."

"Someone at the laboratory," Sofia said, understanding dawning in her eyes. "Someone who had access to the results before they were sent to us."

Sophie's phone buzzed with a message from Nate:

Nate: At the hotel in town. Saw some interesting activity last night—expensive cars, men in suits who didn't look like tourists. Are you safe?

She typed back quickly:

Sophie: We just discovered why Marco was killed. The land contains valuable mineral deposits. Not just valuable, but potentially worth tens of millions.

Nate: Jesus, Sophie. Do you have proof?

Sophie: Official geological survey. But if the wrong people find out we have it...

Nate: Get out of there. Now. Come to the hotel. I've got a room where we can figure this out safely.

Sophie showed the messages to Sofia and Antonio, watching their faces go pale as they absorbed the implications.

"He's right," Antonio said, standing abruptly. "If Vincenzo realizes we have the survey results, he'll escalate. We've seen what he's willing to do to protect his interests."

Sofia was studying the geological report with growing intensity. "Look at this map showing where the samples were taken. The highest concentrations are right along the disputed boundary—exactly where those wartime documents are supposedly buried."

Sophie felt the pieces clicking together with frightening clarity. "The documents aren't just about family shame or collaboration. They're about mineral rights that have been hidden since the 1940s."

"Which means," Antonio continued grimly, "whoever controls those documents controls access to potentially hundreds of millions of dollars in mineral wealth."

Before they could discuss their next move, the sound of vehicles approaching made them all freeze. Through the window, Sophie could see multiple cars coming up the drive—Vincenzo's familiar sedan followed by two larger vehicles that could only belong to security personnel.

"Hide the report," Sofia said urgently.

Sophie looked around desperately, then remembered her successful hiding place from the day before. She quickly moved to the old bread oven built into the kitchen fireplace, wrapping the geological survey in a kitchen towel and shoving it deep behind the cold stone where she'd hidden Marco's documents.

"Whatever happens," she said to Sofia and Antonio, "don't let them know we've seen the test results."

A confident knock echoed through the house, followed by Vincenzo's voice calling out with false friendliness.

"Sofia! Antonio! I hope you don't mind the early visit, but we have some urgent matters to discuss."

Sofia exchanged a look with her brother before moving toward the front door. Sophie stayed in the kitchen, positioning herself where she could hear but remain out of sight.

Vincenzo entered with Dr. Sardelli and two men Sophie didn't recognize—both carrying themselves like security professionals, their eyes constantly scanning for threats or escape routes.

"I trust you all recovered well from the festival," Vincenzo said smoothly. "Such a wonderful celebration of tradition, though I noticed some... tension in the community."

"People are still grieving *Nonno*," Sofia replied carefully. "It's a difficult time."

"Of course, of course. Which is why I wanted to discuss some opportunities that might help ease the family's transition." Vincenzo's tone was warm, but his eyes remained cold and calculating. "I understand you've been conducting some research into the property's characteristics?"

Sophie felt her blood turn to ice. He knew about the geological survey.

Antonio's voice was carefully controlled when he responded. "What kind of research?"

"Soil analysis, geological surveys—the sort of comprehensive study any responsible property owner might undertake." Dr. Sardelli stepped forward, his manner scholarly but menacing. "We've heard that your grandfather commissioned some rather extensive testing before his untimely death."

Sofia's hands clenched at her sides. "I don't know what you're talking about."

"Come now," Vincenzo said with practiced patience. "We're all sophisticated people here. Marco was a careful man who understood the importance of proper documentation. I'm sure he shared his findings with family members he trusted."

One of the security men moved closer to Antonio, close enough to be intimidating without being overtly threatening. "Sometimes families inherit more than they realize," he said in accented English. "Information can be just as valuable as property."

Sophie remained frozen in the kitchen, her mind racing through their options. They were outnumbered, outgunned, and dealing with people who had already committed murder to protect their interests.

"I think there's been a misunderstanding," Antonio said, his voice betraying only the slightest tremor. "If *Nonno* commissioned any surveys, we haven't received the results."

Vincenzo smiled, but it didn't reach his eyes. "How unfortunate. Though I should mention that certain laboratories have been experiencing... security issues recently. Important documents going missing, results being delayed or misdirected. Such an unreliable world we live in."

The threat was clear—they had people inside the laboratory, people who could intercept or alter any inconvenient findings.

Dr. Sardelli produced a folder from his briefcase. "Perhaps we could help resolve this uncertainty. We've taken the liberty of commissioning our own geological analysis of the area. The results are... illuminating."

He spread several documents on the kitchen table—official-looking reports with impressive seals and signatures. Sophie couldn't see the details from her hiding spot, but the family's silence suggested the documents contained information that confirmed their worst fears.

"As you can see," Vincenzo continued, "your property sits on some rather unique geological formations. The kind that might require specialized development to unlock their full potential."

"Development?" Sofia's voice was tight with controlled anger.

"Mining operations," Dr. Sardelli said bluntly. "Properly managed, of course, with full attention to environmental concerns and community impact. But the mineral deposits beneath your olive groves could transform this entire region's economy."

Antonio's chair scraped against the floor as he stood. "You want to strip-mine our family's land."

"We want to create a partnership that benefits everyone," Vincenzo corrected smoothly. "Your family would retain ownership while we handle the technical aspects of resource extraction. Everyone profits."

"And if we refuse?" Sofia asked.

One of the security men shifted position, his jacket falling open just enough to reveal a shoulder holster. "That would be unfortunate. Especially given the legal complexities surrounding mineral rights and wartime property transfers."

Sophie felt her heart pounding as she realized they were witnessing the same pressure tactics that had likely led to Marco's murder. The old man had refused to cooperate, so they'd eliminated him and now were applying direct pressure to his survivors.

Her phone vibrated silently with another message from Nate:

> Nate: Sophie, are you all right? I can see multiple vehicles at the farmhouse from town.

> SHE TEXTED BACK AS QUIETLY AS POSSIBLE:

> Sophie: Vincenzo is here with security. They know about the mineral deposits. Need help.

> Nate: On my way. Stall them if you can.

"We need time to consider your proposal," Antonio said, his voice steadier than Sophie expected.

"Of course," Vincenzo replied. "Though I should mention that time is somewhat limited. Other parties have expressed interest in the region's resources, and regulatory environments can change quickly. It would be a shame if bureaucratic delays prevented your family from benefiting from their inheritance."

Dr. Sardelli closed his folder with decisive finality.

"We'll need an answer within forty-eight hours. After that, we may need to explore alternative approaches to resource development."

As the men prepared to leave, Vincenzo paused at the door, his gaze sweeping the kitchen as if he could sense the hidden documents by pure will.

"Oh, and Sofia," he said casually, "I hope you'll mention to Miss Brooks that her blog posts about local traditions have been... noticed. Sometimes outside perspectives can be misinterpreted, especially when they involve sensitive local matters."

After they left, Sophie emerged from the kitchen to find Sofia and Antonio standing in stunned silence, the weight of the confrontation settling over them like a suffocating blanket.

"They're going to kill us," Sofia said quietly. "All of us. Just like they killed *Nonno*."

"Not if we expose them first," Sophie replied grimly. "We have proof now—the real geological survey, Marco's journal, evidence of their intimidation tactics."

Antonio shook his head. "Proof doesn't matter if we're dead before we can use it."

Sophie's phone rang, and she answered Nate's call with relief.

"Where are you?" his voice was tight with concern.

"Still at the farmhouse. They just left, but Nate—this is bigger than we imagined. The mineral deposits could be worth hundreds of millions. This isn't just about local development anymore."

"I'm five minutes out. Get whatever evidence you have and be ready to move. We need to get you somewhere safe while we figure out how to expose this."

As Sophie hung up, she looked at Sofia and Antonio, seeing the fear and determination warring in their expressions. They'd uncovered the truth about Marco's murder and the conspiracy to steal their land, but now they had to survive long enough to bring that truth to light.

"Get the documents from the bread oven," she said to Sofia. "We're leaving."

The harvest of truth was entering its most dangerous phase.

Now came the pressing. Secrets. Soil. The truth. And someone would be crushed.

---

*FROM SOPHIE'S SUBSTACK: **Farm-to-Table Adventures***

"Today I learned that the most valuable crops aren't always the ones that grow above ground. Beneath Tuscany's olive groves lie treasures that men will kill for—rare earth elements that power our modern world. Marco died protecting more than family tradition. He died protecting Italy's future from those who would sell it to the highest bidder..."

CHAPTER 12
COUNTDOWN TO MIDNIGHT

SOPHIE STOOD at the farmhouse window, the wrapped geological survey and Marco's journal clutched to her chest. Out in the night, every sound made her pulse jump—the crunch of gravel, the groan of shifting branches, the distant hum of an engine.

Headlights finally swept across the courtyard. Relief flooded her as Nate's rental car pulled up, dust swirling around it like smoke. She didn't wait for him to knock. Sophie pushed open the door and hurried outside, heart pounding with something more than fear.

Nate climbed out of the driver's seat, looking different somehow—more serious than the easy-going restaurant owner she'd left in Sonoma, but with the same warmth in his eyes that had drawn her months ago.

"Sophie." He reached her before she'd even made it down the steps, pulling her into a fierce hug that smelled of familiar cologne and travel stress. For a moment, she allowed herself to sink into the solid comfort of his presence.

Behind her, Sofia and Antonio emerged with their bags, casting wary glances at the shadows that pressed against the farmhouse walls. Tonight, they wouldn't be staying here. Tonight, Nate would drive them somewhere safer.

"You came," she said against his shoulder.

"Did you really think I wouldn't?" He pulled back to study her face, his expression darkening as he took in the strain around her eyes. "Jesus, Sophie. When I got your messages about murder and mineral deposits, I thought you were exaggerating."

"I wish I was." She gestured to Sofia and Antonio, who were hanging back respectfully. "Nate, meet Sofia and Antonio De Luca. Their grandfather was Marco."

Nate's expression sobered immediately as he shook their hands. "I'm sorry for your loss. Sophie's told me what an extraordinary man he was."

"*Grazie*," Sofia said quietly. "And thank you for coming. We need all the allies we can get."

Nate's hotel room was small but clean, with windows overlooking the ancient city walls. Sophie felt marginally safer behind the locked door, though she knew their enemies had resources that wouldn't be stopped by simple hotel security.

"Show me what you've got," Nate said, settling into the room's single chair while the others arranged themselves on the bed and small couch.

Sophie spread out Marco's journal, the geological survey, and her phone with the photos of Vincenzo's forged documents. As she walked Nate through every-thing they'd discovered—the mineral deposits, the wartime connections, the decades-long conspiracy—she watched his expression grow increasingly grim.

"This is industrial espionage on a massive scale," he said finally. "Sophie, these people aren't just local criminals. If they're sitting on hundreds of millions in rare earth deposits, they've got international connections, probably government ties."

Antonio leaned forward, his earlier panic replaced by growing determination. "You're saying we're not just fighting a developer. We're fighting a mining corporation."

"At minimum," Nate confirmed. "Rare earth elements are strategically important—countries go to war over access to these materials. If word gets out about deposits this size in Italy, you'll have Chinese companies, American tech giants, and European governments all trying to get a piece."

Sofia paled. "No wonder they killed *Nonno*. He wasn't just refusing to sell farmland—he was standing in the way of geopolitical interests."

Antonio rubbed his hands over his face. "And we're supposed to fight that? With blog posts and press releases?"

"With truth," Sophie said. "And people who believe in it."

Sophie's phone buzzed with a message from an unknown number:

Unknown: You have something that belongs to us. Return it within 6 hours, or your new boyfriend will join the old man.

Sophie showed the message to the group, watching Nate's jaw tighten as he absorbed the threat.

"They're tracking us," she said. "They know you're here, know we're together."

"Then we need to move fast," Nate replied. "What's your plan?"

Sophie looked around the room at the faces watching her—Sofia's grief mixed with determination, Antonio's newfound resolve, Nate's steady competence. Just a few months ago, she'd been a food blogger running from her own problems. Now she was leading a group against killers who had international backing.

"We expose everything," she said. "The mineral survey, Marco's murder, Vincenzo's conspiracy—all of it. But we need to do it in a way that protects us from retaliation."

"How?" Antonio asked.

Sophie pulled out her laptop. "My blog has fifty thousand subscribers across Europe and North America. If I publish everything—with documentation—it becomes international news. They can't kill all of us if the whole world is watching."

Nate nodded approvingly. "Public exposure is your best protection. But you need to be thorough—once you publish, there's no taking it back."

"There's something else," Sofia said quietly. "The olive harvest festival starts again tonight—the second day. The whole community will be there, including the regional press. If we time the blog post to coincide with a public announcement..."

"Maximum impact," Sophie finished. "They can't suppress a story that's already gone viral."

Antonio stood, pacing to the window. "It's risky. Once we make this public, there's no going back to our quiet lives."

"*Nonno* didn't have the luxury of going back," Sofia

replied firmly. "They killed him to steal our heritage. We owe him justice."

Sophie began typing, crafting the most important blog post of her career. Her blog had once celebrated olive oil and tradition. Now it was an indictment. A manifesto.

FROM SOPHIE'S SUBSTACK: Farm-to-Table Adventures

"I came to Tuscany to write about olive oil. Instead, I discovered a conspiracy that reaches from ancient family feuds to modern geopolitical warfare. Marco De Luca died protecting more than olive trees—he died defending Italy's mineral wealth from those who would strip-mine it for profit while hiding behind shell companies and forged documents..."

As she wrote, weaving together Marco's journal entries, the geological evidence, and her own investigative discoveries, Sophie felt the familiar thrill of pursuing truth. But this time, the stakes were life and death.

"How long until you can publish?" Nate asked, reading over her shoulder.

"Two hours to write it properly, another hour to format everything with the supporting documents." Sophie's fingers flew over the keyboard. "The festival starts up again at sunset—if we time this right, I can publish just as Sofia makes her announcement to the crowd."

Sofia's phone rang, making everyone freeze. She glanced at the screen and frowned. "It's Elena from the market. I should answer—if I don't, it'll seem suspicious."

"*Pronto*, Elena," Sofia said, putting the call on speaker so they could all hear.

"Sofia, *cara*, where are you? People are asking about your family's participation in tonight's festival."

"We'll be there," Sofia replied carefully. "We want to honor *Nonno's* memory."

"*Bene*. But Sofia... there are strangers asking questions about you at the market. Men with expensive clothes who don't look like tourists. Be careful."

After Elena hung up, the room fell silent. Their enemies were closing in, but they were also running out of time to act.

"We stick to the plan," Sophie said, her voice steadier than she felt. "I finish the blog post, we go to the festival, Sofia makes the announcement about Marco's murder, and I publish everything simultaneously."

"And if Vincenzo's people try to stop us?" Antonio asked.

Nate reached into his travel bag and withdrew something that made Sophie's eyes widen—a small digital recorder and what looked like a professional-grade camera with a telephoto lens.

"I wasn't entirely honest about why I came to Italy," he said with a slight smile. "I've been consulting with some investigative journalists who've been tracking international mining corruption. When Sophie told me about rare earth deposits and suspicious deaths, a few alarm bells went off."

Sophie stared at him. "You're not just here to rescue me. You're here to document this."

"Both," Nate confirmed. "Sophie, this story is bigger than your blog. If we can get solid evidence of the conspiracy, we can expose an entire network of resource theft that's been operating across Europe."

Sofia leaned forward with interest. "What kind of evidence?"

"Audio recordings of threats, photos of the intimidation, documentation of the forged geological surveys—anything that proves criminal conspiracy." Nate's expression grew more serious. "But I have to warn you, once we start gathering evidence actively, we become even bigger targets."

Sophie's phone buzzed again—this time with a message from Oliver:

> Oliver: Darling, your last blog post about "family tensions" has me worried. Are you sure you're not in over your head?
> Because if you need an extraction, I know people in Rome who owe me favors. ✈️

She typed back quickly:

Sophie: More over my head than you know. Publishing something big tonight that could change everything. If you don't hear from me by midnight, call the authorities.

> Oliver: SOPHIE. That's not reassuring. What exactly are you planning?

> Sophie: Exposing a conspiracy involving murder and mineral theft. The kind that gets people killed for knowing too much.

> Oliver: Goodness, Sophie. This isn't amateur sleuthing anymore—it's a freaking spy novel. Do not be a martyr. I mean it.

Sophie: I promise. But Oliver, if something happens to me, make sure this story gets told. The truth matters more than my safety.

As Sophie set her phone aside, she caught Nate watching her with an expression she couldn't quite read.

"Second thoughts about coming to Italy?" she asked.

"About coming to Italy? Never." His voice was quiet but firm. "About letting you walk into danger? Every minute."

Their eyes met across the small room, and Sophie felt the familiar flutter of connection she'd been trying to ignore since his arrival. Whatever was happening between them—friendship, attraction, something deeper—it would have to wait until they survived the next few hours.

"The festival starts in three hours," Sofia said, checking her phone. "We should prepare for whatever Vincenzo might try."

As the afternoon wore on and Sophie polished her exposé, she couldn't shake the feeling that they were walking into a trap. But sometimes, she reflected, the only way out of a trap was to spring it yourself—and hope you were faster than the people who'd set it.

Tonight, they'd scatter truth like seeds at harvest. With luck, something just might take root before the earth swallowed them too.

FROM SOPHIE'S SUBSTACK: *Farm-to-Table Adventures (DRAFT)*

"Marco De Luca died protecting secrets buried in Tuscan soil

for eighty years. Tonight, those secrets will finally see daylight. Some harvests are worth dying for. Others are worth killing for. The question is: which side of that line are you willing to stand on?"

CHAPTER 13
THE CONTRACT

THE LATE AFTERNOON sun cast long shadows through the hotel room windows as Sophie put the finishing touches on her exposé. Her laptop screen glowed with what she knew would be the most important piece of writing she'd ever publish—a detailed account of Marco's murder, the mineral conspiracy, and Vincenzo's network of corruption that stretched across international borders.

"It's ready," she announced, looking up from the screen to find three pairs of eyes watching her intently.

Nate leaned over to read the final paragraphs, his expression growing more impressed with each sentence. "This is investigative journalism at its finest, Sophie. You've connected all the dots—the wartime documents, the mineral rights, the systematic intimidation of local families."

Sofia wiped tears from her eyes as she finished reading Marco's journal entries that Sophie had quoted. "You captured his voice perfectly. He would be proud to know his words will finally expose these criminals."

Before anyone could respond, Antonio's phone rang. He glanced at the screen and frowned. "It's Elena again. Should I answer?"

"Put it on speaker," Sophie said, her instincts warning her that another call from the market vendor might not be coincidental.

"Pronto, Elena," Antonio said carefully.

"Antonio, thank God I reached you." Elena's voice was strained with barely controlled panic. "You need to know —I've been forced to tell them where you are."

The hotel room went silent except for the sound of everyone's sharp intake of breath.

"Forced how?" Sofia demanded.

"They have my grandson," Elena's voice broke. "Little Marco—they took him from school an hour ago. They say they'll hurt him if I don't cooperate."

Sophie felt her blood turn to ice. Using a child as leverage was an escalation that proved just how desperate Vincenzo's organization had become.

"Elena, where are they holding him?" Nate asked, his voice tight with controlled anger.

"I don't know. They just showed me a photo of him crying, said they'd return him safely if I told them where you were staying and convinced you to meet with them."

Antonio gripped the phone so hard his knuckles went white. "What do they want?"

"A trade. The geological survey and Marco's journal in exchange for little Marco's safety. They want to meet at the old grain mill outside town in one hour."

Sophie and Nate exchanged a look that communicated volumes. It was obviously a trap—but what choice did they have with a child's life at stake?

"Elena, we'll figure something out," Sofia said. "Keep your phone on, and don't do anything else they ask until you hear from us."

After Elena hung up, the room erupted in urgent discussion.

"We can't just hand over the evidence," Antonio said. "Without it, we have no way to prove what they've done."

"And we can't let them hurt that child," Sofia replied fiercely. "Little Marco is eight years old—this isn't his fight."

Sophie was already thinking through their options, her mind working with the clarity that came from months of solving problems under pressure. "We don't have to choose between the evidence and the child's safety. But we need to be smart about this."

"What do you mean?" Nate asked.

Sophie turned her laptop screen toward them, showing the publish button for her blog post. "I can schedule this to go live automatically in two hours. That gives us time to attempt the exchange, but ensures the truth gets out regardless of what happens to us."

"That's assuming they don't just kill all of us once they have what they want," Antonio pointed out grimly.

"Which is why we're not going to that grain mill," Nate said. "At least, not the way they expect."

Sophie raised an eyebrow. "What are you thinking?"

Nate pulled out his professional camera and the small recording device he'd shown them earlier. "I scout the location first, document whatever security they've set up, and look for the child. Meanwhile, you three go to the festival as planned and proceed with the public announcement."

"That's too dangerous," Sophie protested. "You could be walking into an ambush."

"Someone has to." Nate's expression was resolute. "If little Marco is really there, he needs an adult who can get him to safety. And if it's a trap, better that one of us walks into it knowingly than all of us walk into it blind."

Sofia was studying a map on her phone. "The old grain mill is only two kilometers from the festival site. If we time everything right..."

"I make the announcement about Marco's murder and the mineral conspiracy just as my blog post goes live," Sophie finished. "Maximum exposure, maximum protection."

Antonio looked unconvinced. "And if they retaliate by hurting Elena's grandson?"

"Then we make sure they don't get the chance," Nate said grimly. "But Antonio, these people killed your grandfather. They're not going to suddenly develop a conscience just because we cooperate."

Sophie felt the weight of the decision settling on her shoulders. In the past, she'd always been reactive—responding to Ryan's betrayal, fleeing to Sonoma, investigating Marco's death after it happened. Now she was being proactive, making choices that could save lives or get people killed.

"There's something else we need to consider," she said slowly. "The wartime documents that Paolo mentioned—the ones supposedly buried near the boundary stone. If they're real, they might contain information about the original mineral surveys from the 1940s."

Nate looked up sharply. "You think that's what this is

really about? Not just the current deposits, but historical claims to them?"

"Think about it," Sophie continued. "Italian mineral rights law is complex, especially for anything discovered during wartime. If there are documents proving that the Fascist government or the German occupation identified these deposits, it could affect who has a legal claim to them now."

Sofia's eyes widened as she understood the implications. "So Vincenzo isn't just stealing our family's land—he's potentially stealing state resources that should belong to the Italian people."

"Which makes this a matter of national security," Antonio added. "No wonder they're willing to commit murder to keep it quiet."

Sophie's phone buzzed with a message from Ryan:

Ryan: Sophie, I've heard through mutual contacts that you might be in trouble. If you need help, I can be back in Montepulciano by tonight.

She stared at the message, remembering the lies and betrayal that had ended their marriage. But she also remembered that beneath his flaws, Ryan had connections in international business that might prove useful.

"My ex-husband," she explained to the others. "He's offering to help."

"Can you trust him?" Nate asked, and Sophie caught the slight edge in his voice.

"I can trust him to act in his own self-interest," Sophie replied. "The question is whether helping us serves that interest."

She typed back carefully:

Sophie: You've always claimed your work gives you an

ear for shady deals. How much do you actually know about Vincenzo Rossi?

Ryan: You already know I've crossed paths with Rossi. What matters is why I kept tabs on him. His name keeps surfacing in connection with suspicious geological surveys and mineral rights disputes. That's the kind of thing I track for my clients—and for myself. When I realized his operations overlapped with Tuscany, I started paying closer attention. If Rossi falls, someone else stands to gain —and I intend to make sure I'm not left out.

Sophie showed the message to the group, watching their expressions shift from suspicion to intrigued surprise.

"He knows about Vincenzo?" Sofia asked.

"Apparently." Sophie typed another response: "How much do you know about rare earth mining fraud in Italy?"

Ryan's reply came quickly: "Enough to know that several American tech companies have been burned by deals involving non-existent mineral deposits and forged geological surveys. Enough to know that Vincenzo Rossi is suspected of defrauding investors out of hundreds of millions across multiple countries."

The pieces clicked together in Sophie's mind with star-tling clarity. "He's not just a local developer. Vincenzo is running an international mineral rights scam, and your family's land might be one of the few places where the deposits are actually real."

Sophie's fingers flew over her phone keyboard: "Ryan, are you willing to provide testimony about Vincenzo's fraud to Italian authorities?"

"Already on my way back to Montepulciano," came the

reply. "If you can prove he's operating in Tuscany, I can connect his activities to fraudulent deals in six other countries. This could bring down his entire network."

Nate was staring at Sophie's phone with undisguised skepticism. "He swoops in at the eleventh hour and gets to play the white knight?" he murmured.

As the sun began to set outside their hotel window, Sophie felt the familiar mix of terror and exhilaration that came with pursuing a story larger than she'd imagined. What had started as a food blog about olive oil had become an international investigation into mineral rights fraud, murder, and governmental corruption.

"Change of plans," she announced to the group. "Nate still scouts the grain mill and looks for Elena's grandson. Sofia and Antonio go to the festival and prepare for the public announcement. But instead of just publishing my blog post, we coordinate with Ryan to provide evidence to both Italian authorities and international law enforcement simultaneously."

"And you?" Sofia asked.

Sophie looked at her laptop screen, where her exposé waited to be published to fifty thousand subscribers around the world. "I make sure this story reaches every journalist, every law enforcement agency, and every government official who needs to see it. By midnight tonight, Vincenzo's conspiracy will be international news."

Nate stood, checking his camera equipment and recording devices. "If this works, we save the child, expose the conspiracy, and bring down an international criminal network."

"And if it doesn't work?" Antonio asked.

Sophie met his gaze steadily. "Then at least the truth dies with us, not before us."

As they prepared to leave the hotel room—possibly for the last time—Sophie felt the weight of Marco's trust and the responsibility of the story she was about to tell. The old man had died protecting secrets. Now it was time to make sure those secrets served justice instead of greed.

The festival lights were beginning to twinkle in the distance, and somewhere in the Tuscan countryside, a child waited to be rescued and a conspiracy waited to be exposed.

The harvest was about to reach its climax, and Sophie was ready to press every drop of truth from the bitter fruit of secrets that had been too long buried in Italian soil.

---

*From Sophie's Substack: **Farm-to-Table Adventures***

"SCHEDULED TO PUBLISH: In one hour, this post will expose a conspiracy that reaches from Tuscan olive groves to international boardrooms. Marco De Luca died protecting Italy's mineral wealth from those who would steal it. Tonight, his killers face justice. The truth, like olives under pressure, yields its essence only when the pressing becomes unbearable."

CHAPTER 14
PRESSING THE TRUTH

THE ANCIENT STONE streets of Montepulciano echoed with the sounds of preparation as vendors set up for the second night of the olive harvest festival. Sophie watched from the hotel window as locals hung garlands of olive branches between medieval buildings and arranged tables laden with the season's bounty. The scene should have been picturesque, but knowing that somewhere in the countryside a child was being held hostage cast a dark shadow over the celebration.

"Radio check," Nate's voice crackled through the small communications device he'd given her before leaving for the grain mill. The equipment was military-grade, something he'd acquired through his mysterious investigative contacts.

"Clear reception," Sophie replied, testing the nearly invisible earpiece. "How far out are you?"

"Ten minutes from the mill. I can see tire tracks in the dirt—recent ones. Multiple vehicles." His voice was tense but controlled. "Sophie, if this goes sideways, you publish that blog post immediately. Don't wait for the scheduled time."

"Understood." Sophie checked her laptop one more time, confirming that her exposé was ready to launch with a single keystroke. She'd added Ryan's information about Vincenzo's international fraud network, creating a document that would simultaneously alert law enforcement agencies across six countries.

Sofia appeared at Sophie's elbow, dressed in the traditional festival clothing she'd worn to honor her grandfather—a simple but elegant black dress with an olive branch pin that had belonged to her grandmother. "The festival organizers are expecting our announcement in thirty minutes. The press will be there, regional television, even some international food writers who came for the traditional pressing demonstration."

"Perfect timing," Antonio said, adjusting his own festival attire. He looked more composed than he had since Elena's devastating phone call, but Sophie could see the tension in the set of his shoulders. "If we're going to make this public, we need maximum exposure."

Sophie's phone buzzed with a message from Ryan:

> Ryan: Coordinating with Italian financial crimes unit and Interpol. They're very interested in Vincenzo's activities. Where should I meet you?

SHE TYPED BACK:

> Sophie: Main piazza, near the olive pressing demonstration. Look for the woman about to accuse a major developer of murder.

Ryan: Jesus, Sophie. Are you sure about this approach? Once you make public accusations, there's no taking them back.

Sophie: Marco De Luca deserves justice. And Elena's grandson deserves to come home safely.

As they prepared to leave the hotel, Sophie caught sight of herself in the mirror. She looked different than she had three months ago in Sonoma—more confident, more purposeful, but also marked by the weight of the secrets she carried. Her camera hung around her neck, ready to document whatever happened next.

"You know," she said to Sofia and Antonio, "when I started this food blog, I thought I'd be writing about olive oil and traditional recipes."

"Instead, you became an investigative journalist," Sofia replied with a sad smile. "Perhaps that's what you were meant to be all along."

"Perhaps." Sophie shouldered her laptop bag, feeling the weight of Marco's journal and the geological survey safely stored inside. "But I'd rather have met your grandfather under happier circumstances."

They made their way through the narrow streets toward the festival, joining streams of locals and tourists heading for the celebration. The atmosphere was festive but Sophie's trained eye caught signs of tension—too many men in expensive suits for a agricultural festival, subtle positioning that suggested security rather than casual attendance, the kind of watchful alertness that meant professional observers.

"Vincenzo's people," Antonio murmured, noticing her

scrutiny.

"Good," Sophie replied grimly. "That means they're taking us seriously."

The main piazza had been transformed into a showcase of traditional Tuscan agriculture. Tables displayed bottles of newly pressed olive oil, wheels of local cheese, and baskets of preserved olives that gleamed like jewels in the early evening light. At the center of the square, a restored antique olive press had been set up for demonstration purposes—the same type of equipment Marco's family had used for generations.

Sophie felt her phone vibrate with Nate's voice in her earpiece: "I'm at the mill. There's definitely someone here —I can see movement inside the building. Two vehicles parked outside, possibly more around back."

"Be careful," she whispered, positioning herself near a food stall where she could speak without being overheard.

"Always am. Sophie... if something happens to me tonight, make sure this story gets told."

"Nothing's going to happen to you," she replied firmly, though her heart was racing.

"I can see the kid," Nate's voice came through more urgently. "He's tied up in what looks like an office, crying but appears unharmed. I count at least four adults—three men, one woman. Professional setup."

Sophie's blood ran cold at the confirmation that Elena's grandson was really there. Whatever else happened tonight, they had to get that child to safety.

"Festival organizers are starting the announcements," Sofia said, approaching with a microphone in her hand. "Are you ready?"

Sophie looked around the crowded piazza, noting the mixture of faces—locals she recognized from the market, tourists with cameras, journalists with notebooks, and scattered throughout the crowd, Vincenzo's watchers. At the edge of the square, she spotted Ryan arriving with two other men in official-looking suits who could only be law enforcement.

Her phone buzzed with Oliver's voice:

> Oliver: Darling, I've been refreshing your blog every five minutes. When are you publishing this earth-shattering exposé? The suspense is killing me! 🫒 💀

> Sophie: Ten minutes. About to make the announcement that will either save lives or get us all killed.

> Oliver: SOPHIE. That's not the reassuring update I was hoping for. Promise me you have an exit strategy.

> Sophie: Working on it. If you don't hear from me by tomorrow, call every journalist you know and make sure this story gets told.

> Oliver: I love you, you magnificent, terrifying woman. Don't you dare become a martyr for olive oil.

The festival coordinator took the makeshift stage—a wooden platform erected in front of the ancient olive press. "Ladies and gentlemen, we gather tonight to celebrate not just the harvest, but the traditions that have sustained our community for generations. Tonight, we honor those who have preserved these traditions, including our dear friend Marco De Luca, whose recent passing reminds us that we must never take these gifts for granted."

A murmur of respectful agreement ran through the crowd. Sophie saw several people cross themselves or nod solemnly at Marco's name.

"However," the coordinator continued, "before we begin the traditional pressing demonstration, Signora Sofia De Luca has asked to make a special announcement regarding her grandfather's legacy."

Sofia stepped onto the platform, and Sophie felt a surge of pride at her friend's courage. In the space of a week, Sofia had lost her grandfather, discovered his murder, and now was preparing to publicly accuse powerful people of conspiracy and killing. The quiet woman who managed agriturismo guests had transformed into someone willing to risk everything for justice.

"Thank you," Sofia began, her voice carrying clearly across the square. "Many of you knew my grandfather, Marco De Luca. You knew him as a man who loved this land, who preserved traditions that stretch back centuries, who believed that the way we treat the earth reflects who we are as people."

Nods and murmurs of agreement from the crowd. Sophie noticed movement among Vincenzo's watchers— they were positioning themselves closer to the stage, clearly preparing to intervene if necessary.

"What you may not know," Sofia continued, her voice growing stronger, "is that my grandfather did not die in an accident. Marco De Luca was murdered."

The crowd fell silent, shocked gasps and murmurs

rippling through the gathered people. Several journalists immediately pulled out phones and recorders.

"He was murdered by people who saw our family's land not as agricultural heritage, but as a source of mineral wealth to be exploited. People who were willing to kill an eighty-three-year-old man rather than accept his refusal to sell."

Sophie's heart pounded as she watched the crowd's reaction. Some faces showed shock and disbelief, others anger, but she could see that Sofia's words were landing with the force of truth.

Nate's voice crackled urgently in her earpiece: "Sophie, something's happening here. Vehicles are leaving the mill, heading toward town fast. I think they're abandoning the location."

"Did you get the child?" she whispered.

"Working on it. Keep going with the announcement—I think your plan is working. They're panicking."

Sofia was continuing her speech, her voice now carrying the passionate anger that had been building for days. "The man responsible for my grandfather's death is here tonight, in this very crowd. Vincenzo Rossi has spent decades stealing mineral wealth from Italian families, using murder and intimidation to—"

She was interrupted by commotion at the edge of the crowd. Vincenzo himself was pushing through the gathered people, flanked by Dr. Sardelli and several security personnel. His usual polished composure had cracked, revealing desperate fury underneath.

"Enough!" he shouted, climbing onto the platform. "This woman is clearly distraught by grief. These wild accusations—"

"Are backed by documentary evidence," Sophie announced, stepping forward with her laptop. She had opened the device and her finger hovered over the publish button. "Evidence that I'm uploading to the internet right now."

The crowd turned to stare at her, and Sophie felt the familiar rush of adrenaline that came with being at the center of a story. "My name is Sophie Brooks, and I'm an investigative journalist. For the past week, I've been documenting a conspiracy involving mineral rights fraud, international money laundering, and the murder of Marco De Luca."

She hit the publish button.

Across the square, she could see Ryan and his law enforcement colleagues moving purposefully through the crowd, their official credentials visible as they approached Vincenzo's position.

"The evidence is now public," Sophie announced to the crowd, many of whom were frantically checking their phones as her blog post appeared online. "Geological surveys proving valuable mineral deposits under the De Luca property, documents showing Vincenzo's fraud network across six countries, and Marco's own journal entries documenting threats against his family."

Vincenzo's face had gone pale, but he made one last desperate play. "You have no idea what you've done," he snarled at Sophie. "There are things at stake here that you don't understand. People who won't tolerate this interference."

"I understand perfectly," Sophie replied. "You're a criminal who kills elderly men for their land and kidnaps children to cover your tracks."

The accusation about kidnapping was a calculated risk, but Sophie saw it land—Vincenzo's eyes flickered with surprise and guilt, confirming that Elena's grandson had indeed been taken by his organization.

Dr. Sardelli stepped forward, his scholarly demeanor finally cracking. "You don't know what forces you're dealing with," he said menacingly. "This goes beyond local business—"

He was interrupted by Ryan's arrival with Italian financial crimes investigators. "Vincenzo Rossi, you're under arrest for fraud, conspiracy, and suspicion of murder. Dr. Sardelli, you're also under arrest as an accessory."

The crowd erupted in confused chatter as handcuffs appeared and official badges were displayed. Sophie felt a surge of triumph mixed with relief—they had done it. The conspiracy was exposed, the criminals were being arrested, and the truth was spreading across the internet.

Nate's voice crackled through her earpiece with the news she'd been hoping for: "Got him. The kid is safe, in my car, and we're heading back to town. Elena can stop worrying."

Sophie nearly collapsed with relief. Little Marco was safe, the truth was public, and justice was finally being served.

But as the Italian police led Vincenzo and Dr. Sardelli away, the developer caught Sophie's eye one last time. His expression carried a promise that chilled her despite the evening's victory—this might be over, but there would be consequences she hadn't yet imagined.

For now, though, truth had triumphed. As the traditional olive pressing demonstration began and the crowd slowly returned to celebration, Sophie felt the satisfaction of a story well told and justice properly served.

Her phone buzzed with messages from around the world as her blog post spread across social media. Oliver, of course, was first:

> Oliver: SOPHIE! You magnificent, dangerous woman! The story is everywhere—BBC, CNN, La Repubblica! You've just exposed an international crime syndicate with a food blog! I'm so proud and terrified for your safety! 🌍✨🌍

As the ancient olive press began its rhythmic work, crushing fruit that had been growing since Marco was a young man, Sophie felt the deep satisfaction of secrets finally exposed to light. The harvest was complete, the truth had been pressed from bitter circumstances, and Tuscany was safe from those who would exploit its treasures.

Tomorrow would bring new challenges, new stories, new destinations. But tonight, in a medieval piazza filled with olive oil and justice, Sophie Brooks had found exactly what she'd been searching for without knowing it—her purpose as a writer, an investigator, and a woman brave enough to fight for what mattered.

The olives weren't the only thing being pressed in Tuscany. And unlike Vincenzo's schemes, the truth would only grow richer with time.

FROM SOPHIE'S SUBSTACK: Farm-to-Table Adventures

"BREAKING: Tonight in Montepulciano, justice was served alongside olive oil. Marco De Luca's murder has been exposed, his killers arrested, and an international mineral fraud conspiracy brought to light. Some harvests take decades to ripen. But when truth is finally pressed from bitter circumstances, it yields the purest oil of all—justice."

CHAPTER 15
THE MORNING AFTER

THE TUSCAN DAWN crept through the farmhouse windows with unusual gentleness, as if even the sun understood that yesterday had been enough drama for a lifetime. Sophie woke to the sound of voices drifting up from the kitchen below—not the urgent, whispered conversations of conspiracy, but the comfortable murmur of people who had survived something together and were learning to breathe again.

She found her phone on the nightstand, blinking with dozens of notifications. Messages from journalists, interview requests from news outlets, comments from readers around the world who had read her exposé. The numbers were staggering—fifty thousand shares in twelve hours, coverage by BBC, CNN, and La Repubblica. Her food blog had become international news.

But what caught her attention was a voicemail from Ryan, timestamped at 3 AM Italian time.

"Sophie... I know I don't deserve another chance, but if this trip has taught me anything, it's that I miss being the person I was with you. I've been watching the news coverage, and I'm proud of what you've accomplished. If you're willing to talk—really talk, about us, about what went wrong—I'll be at Caffè Pitti in Florence tomorrow at noon."

His voice carried the rehearsed quality of someone who had practiced the words, but underneath lay something raw and genuine that reminded her of the man she'd once loved. Before the lies, before the betrayal, before everything had fallen apart in Oregon.

Sophie set the phone aside without responding and made her way downstairs, drawn by the scent of fresh coffee and something sweeter—cornetti warming in the oven, she realized, the Italian equivalent of croissants that Sofia must have picked up from the village bakery.

The kitchen scene that greeted her felt like stepping into a painting of domestic tranquility. Sofia stood at the stove, her dark hair pulled back in a simple bun, stirring something in a small pan that smelled of cinnamon and vanilla. Antonio sat at the old wooden table with a newspaper spread before him, his expression cycling between amazement and worry as he read coverage of their story. Nate occupied the chair beside him, cradling an espresso cup in both hands and looking more relaxed than Sophie had seen him since his arrival.

"*Buongiorno*," Sofia called out without turning around. "Perfect timing. The cornetti are just ready."

Elena appeared from the pantry carrying a jar of what looked like fresh ricotta, her face bright with a kind of peace Sophie hadn't seen before. "Sophie! *Cara mia*, how did you sleep?"

"Better than I expected," Sophie replied honestly, accepting the espresso cup Nate held out to her. Their fingers brushed as she took it, and she felt that familiar flutter of connection, stronger now after everything they'd been through together.

"Any word from Elena's grandson?" she asked.

Elena's face lit up. "Little Marco is perfect. Scared, but safe. He keeps asking if the bad men are really gone forever." Her expression sobered slightly. "I told him yes, but..."

"But you're not entirely sure," Sophie finished gently.

"The mind understands that justice was served," Elena said, settling into a chair with her own coffee. "The heart takes longer to believe in safety."

Sofia placed a platter in the center of the table—warm cornetti split and filled with fresh ricotta, drizzled with honey that caught the morning light like amber. Beside it, she arranged slices of cantaloupe, figs that had been briefly grilled to caramelize their sweetness, and a small bowl of the De Luca's finest olive oil for dipping bread.

"A proper Tuscan breakfast," she announced. "To celebrate being alive."

As they ate, Antonio shared updates from the morning news coverage. "Listen to this headline from Corriere della Sera: 'American Food Blogger Exposes International Mineral Fraud.' And this one from the Financial Times: 'Tuscany Murder Reveals Global Mining Conspiracy.'"

"Don't forget the local paper," Sofia added with dry humor. "They published an editorial questioning whether foreign journalists should involve themselves in Italian family matters."

Sophie felt a familiar pang of uncertainty. "Are people angry that I interfered?"

"Some," Antonio admitted. "But Elena set them straight at the market this morning. Told anyone who'd listen that you saved her grandson and honored our grandfather's memory."

"Besides," Nate added, "the comment threads under your blog post are overwhelmingly supportive. People are calling you a citizen journalist, sharing stories about similar land grabbing in their own communities."

Sophie took a bite of cornetto, savoring the way the sweet ricotta complemented the buttery pastry. "It doesn't feel real yet. Twenty-four hours ago, we were worried about staying alive. Now people are calling me a hero for writing a blog post."

"You did more than write a blog post," Sofia said firmly. "You listened when everyone else wanted to forget. You believed Nonno deserved justice when the authorities were ready to call his death an accident."

Their quiet reflection was interrupted by the sound of a car approaching on the gravel drive. Through the window, Sophie could see a dark sedan with official plates—not the threatening black cars of Vincenzo's organization, but something that suggested legitimate government business.

"Expecting anyone?" Nate asked, his posture automatically straightening.

Sofia shook her head, but her expression wasn't worried—more curious than concerned. "Let me see who it is."

She returned moments later with two people who looked like they'd stepped out of a European crime drama —a woman in her forties with short gray hair and intelligent eyes, and a younger man carrying a leather portfolio. Both wore the kind of understated professional clothing that suggested serious law enforcement credentials.

"Sophie Brooks?" the woman asked, extending her

hand. "I'm Agent Carla Bianchi with Interpol's Financial Crimes division, and this is Agent Marco Rosetti from the Italian Guardia di Finanza. We'd like to speak with you about your investigation into the Rossi organization."

Sophie felt her breakfast settle uneasily in her stomach. "Am I in trouble?"

Agent Bianchi smiled—a genuine expression that eased some of Sophie's tension. "Quite the opposite. Your blog post and supporting documentation have provided crucial evidence for investigations in six countries. We're here to thank you and discuss some follow-up questions."

"Would you like coffee?" Sofia offered, already moving toward the espresso machine. "We can talk here, or if you prefer privacy..."

"Here is fine," Agent Rosetti said, settling into the chair Elena had vacated. "Actually, we're hoping to speak with all of you who were involved. This wasn't just local crime —Vincenzo Rossi's organization has been operating across Europe for over a decade."

As Sofia prepared coffee for the agents, Agent Bianchi opened her portfolio and withdrew several photographs. "Have any of you seen these men before?"

Sophie leaned forward to examine the images—profes- sional headshots that looked like they'd been taken from security cameras or official documents. She didn't recog- nize most of them, but one face made her pause.

"This one," she said, pointing to a man with thinning hair and cold eyes. "He was at the festival last night, standing near Vincenzo during the confrontation."

"Lorenzo Mazzi," Agent Rosetti confirmed. "He managed Rossi's operations in Greece and Turkey. We believe he escaped during last night's arrests, but your identification helps confirm he was active in the Italian operation."

Nate leaned back in his chair, his expression thoughtful. "How extensive was this network?"

"Larger than we initially realized," Agent Bianchi replied. "The mineral rights fraud extended to properties in Greece, Spain, southern France, and parts of Eastern Europe. Families were pressured to sell agricultural land that supposedly contained valuable deposits, but in most cases, the geological surveys were falsified."

"Most cases?" Antonio asked.

"The De Luca property appears to be one of the few where the mineral deposits are actually real," Agent Rosetti explained. "Which made it both more valuable and more dangerous to Rossi's operations."

Sophie thought about Marco's journal, his careful documentation of threats and suspicious behavior. "So he really did die protecting something worth killing for."

"Millions of euros in rare earth elements," Agent Bianchi confirmed. "But more than that—he died protecting the integrity of Italian mineral rights law. If Rossi had succeeded in obtaining those deposits through fraud and intimidation, it would have set a precedent for similar theft across Southern Europe."

The conversation continued for another hour, with the agents asking detailed questions about the timeline of threats, the content of Marco's journal, and Sophie's methodology for gathering evidence. She found herself describing her investigation with growing confidence, realizing that her instincts and observations had been more sophisticated than she'd given herself credit for.

"Your digital documentation was particularly valuable," Agent Bianchi noted. "The photographs of forged geological surveys, the screenshots of threatening messages, the audio recordings from festival confrontation —they provide a clear chain of evidence that will support prosecutions in multiple jurisdictions."

"What happens next?" Sofia asked.

"Vincenzo Rossi and his immediate associates will face trial in Italy for murder, fraud, and conspiracy," Agent Rosetti explained. "But we'll also be pursuing extradition requests for charges in other countries where his organization operated."

"And for us?" Sophie asked.

"You may be asked to provide testimony via video conference for some of the international cases," Agent Bianchi said. "But primarily, we wanted to thank you. It's rare that a civilian investigation provides this level of detailed evidence."

She paused, then added with a slight smile, "Though I have to ask—how did a food blogger develop such thorough investigative instincts?"

Sophie felt Nate's eyes on her as she considered the question. "I think I've always noticed details that don't fit. Flavors that are off, stories that don't match, people who aren't what they seem. I just never applied those skills to anything more serious than restaurant reviews before."

After the agents left, the farmhouse settled back into peaceful quiet. Sofia busied herself with cleaning the breakfast dishes while Antonio returned to reading news coverage. Nate helped Sophie organize her scattered belongings—camera equipment, notebooks, the precious journal that had started everything.

"I keep thinking about what Agent Bianchi said,"

Sophie mused, watching Nate carefully wrap Marco's journal in a clean kitchen towel. "About this being bigger than we realized."

"Does that worry you?" he asked, his hands gentle as he handled the old leather binding.

"A little. But also..." She searched for the right words. "It makes Marco's death feel meaningful. He didn't just die defending his family's land—he died protecting something that mattered to thousands of families across Europe."

Nate finished wrapping the journal and set it carefully in Sophie's luggage. "I wish I could have met him. From everything you've written about him, he sounds like someone who understood that the smallest actions can have the biggest consequences."

Sophie felt tears prick her eyes—not sadness, exactly, but a complex mix of grief and gratitude. "He would have liked you. You both have that quality of paying attention to what matters."

"Speaking of what matters," Nate said carefully, "have you thought about what comes next? I mean, after all this media attention, you could probably write for any publication you wanted."

Sophie's phone buzzed with a notification—another interview request, this one from a major American news network. She glanced at it and set the phone aside without responding.

"Right now, I just want to finish processing what happened here. But Nate... I'm glad you came. I couldn't have done this alone."

"Yes, you could have," he replied with quiet certainty. "But I'm glad I got to see you do it."

Outside, the afternoon sun was warming the olive

groves where Marco had spent his final morning. Sophie could see workers moving among the trees, beginning the harvest that the festival had celebrated. Life was returning to its seasonal rhythms, but she knew that nothing would ever be quite the same.

Her phone chimed again—this time with a message from Oliver:

> Oliver: Darling, I've been fielding interview requests all morning! The BBC wants to know if you're available for their evening program, and someone from Netflix apparently wants to discuss documentary rights? You've become famous! Should I be jealous? 💻

Sophie smiled, typing back:

> Sophie: Fame is overrated. But justice feels pretty good. How are you handling being the best friend of an international crime-fighting food blogger?

> Oliver: Magnificently, obviously. Though I'm demanding a producer credit if this becomes a documentary. "Oliver Chen: The Man Who Kept Sophie Brooks Fed and Sane." Has a nice ring to it, don't you think?

As the afternoon wore on, Sophie found herself checking news coverage and social media responses to her story. The reaction was overwhelmingly positive, but she noticed the undercurrents that Agent Bianchi had warned her about—comments questioning her motives, suggestions that she was exploiting tragedy for personal gain, a few messages that carried an edge of something darker.

One comment in particular made her pause: "Careful, American girl. Some people don't forget, and Italy has a long memory."

It was probably just internet trolling, but something about the phrasing sent a chill down her spine. She showed it to Nate, who frowned as he read.

"Most likely nothing," he said, but his tone carried a note of caution. "But maybe avoid posting your exact location for a while."

As evening approached, Sophie took a walk through the olive groves, needing time to process everything that had happened. The ancient trees stood in their neat rows, unchanged by the human drama that had played out beneath their branches. In the fading light, she could almost imagine Marco walking these paths, checking on trees that had been in his family for generations.

Her phone rang—Sofia's name on the screen.

"Sophie, where are you? Elena is here with her grandson, and he wants to thank you personally."

"On my way," Sophie replied, turning back toward the farmhouse.

She found Elena in the kitchen with a boy of perhaps eight, dark-haired and serious-faced, clinging to his grandmother's hand. When he saw Sophie, his eyes widened with shy recognition.

"You're the lady who saved me," he said in careful English.

Sophie knelt to his eye level. "What's your name?"

"Marco," he said softly. "Like the *signore* who died."

Sophie felt her heart clench. "It's very nice to meet you, Marco. Are you feeling better now?"

He nodded solemnly. "The bad men can't hurt anyone anymore?"

"No," Sophie said firmly. "They can't hurt anyone anymore."

Little Marco reached into his pocket and pulled out a small object—a wooden olive branch, clearly carved by hand. "I made this for you. Nonna Elena taught me."

Sophie accepted the gift with trembling hands. The carving was simple but beautifully crafted, the olive leaves detailed and smooth to the touch.

"Thank you," she said. "I'll treasure it always."

As she stood, Elena embraced her fiercely. "You brought my bambino home," she whispered. "Whatever happens next in your life, you will always have a family here."

Later, as the farmhouse settled into evening quiet, Sophie sat on her bed with her laptop, finally ready to write her first blog post since the exposé. This one would be different—not an investigation or an accusation, but a reflection on the experience of finding justice in unexpected places.

FROM SOPHIE'S SUBSTACK: *Farm-to-Table Adventures*

"The morning after exposing a conspiracy, I woke to the smell of cornetti and fresh coffee—proof that life continues, that healing happens, that communities survive even the darkest revelations. Today I learned that justice tastes like honey and ricotta, sounds like a child's laughter, and feels like the olive

wood carved by grateful hands. Some harvests take generations to ripen. This one was worth the wait."

As she prepared for sleep, Sophie caught sight of her reflection in the window—the same face that had stared back at her in Oregon six months ago, but transformed by confidence and purpose. Tomorrow would bring new decisions about her future, new opportunities, new uncertainties. Oliver had sent a message that a South African chef wanted to collaborate on a market exposé in Cape Town. Sophie hadn't said yes—but she hadn't said no either.

But tonight, in a Tuscan farmhouse surrounded by olive groves and the memory of a man who had died protecting what he loved, Sophie Brooks was exactly where she belonged.

The truth had been harvested, pressed, and shared. And like the finest olive oil, it would only grow more valuable with time.

CHAPTER 16
A FAREWELL AND
A FORK

THE MORNING AIR carried a hint of autumn as Sophie and Nate made their way up the winding road toward the hilltop winery that had once donated cases of wine to Marco's harvest festival. Neither had called it a date— they'd simply agreed that Sophie needed a break from the farmhouse's constant stream of media calls, and Nate wanted to see more of Tuscany before his flight home tomorrow.

But as they walked side by side through the cypress-lined path leading to Tenuta San Giuseppe, Sophie couldn't ignore the weight of unspoken words between them. In twenty-four hours, he'd be on a plane back to Sonoma, and she'd be left to figure out what came next without the steady presence that had anchored her through the most dangerous week of her life.

"Tell me about this place," Nate said, pausing to photograph the view across the valley where morning mist still clung to the olive groves below.

"Marco mentioned it in his journal," Sophie replied,

consulting the notes she'd transcribed. "The Benedetti family has been making wine here for five generations. When Marco's festival started struggling financially a few years ago, they donated enough Brunello to fund the entire celebration."

"The kind of neighbors who understand community," Nate observed, lowering his camera.

"Exactly the kind of people Vincenzo would have destroyed if he'd succeeded."

They were greeted at the winery by Signora Benedetti herself—a woman in her seventies with silver hair braided down her back and hands stained permanently purple from decades of harvests. She recognized Sophie's name immediately when they introduced themselves.

"Ah, the American journalist who saved the De Luca family," she said, embracing Sophie with fierce warmth. "Marco was like a brother to my late husband. What you did for his memory—brava, cara, brava."

She insisted on giving them a private tour of the estate, leading them through ancient cellars carved directly into the hillside where hundreds of bottles lay aging in the cool darkness. The air smelled of oak and time, of patient processes that couldn't be rushed or faked.

"This is why men like Vincenzo will never understand our way of life," Signora Benedetti said, running her hand along a barrel that had been aging wine since before Sophie was born. "They see only immediate profit, not the generations of knowledge required to create something truly valuable."

In the tasting room—a simple stone chamber with windows overlooking the valley—she poured them glasses of Brunello that caught the light like liquid rubies.

Sophie had learned enough about wine in Sonoma to recognize exceptional quality, but this was something else entirely. Each sip carried the essence of the soil, the memory of countless harvests, the patience of people who understood that the best things couldn't be hurried.

"This is extraordinary," Nate said, and Sophie heard genuine reverence in his voice.

"My husband planted these vines in 1973," Signora Benedetti replied. "He said they would not reach their full potential until after he was gone. He was right—the 2015 vintage, from forty-two-year-old vines, finally achieved what he dreamed of."

The conversation reminded Sophie powerfully of Marco, of his insistence that tradition and patience created value that modern methods could never replicate. She found herself thinking about her own journey—how six months ago, she'd been desperate for immediate solutions to her broken marriage and shattered confidence. Now she understood that some kinds of healing, like good wine, required time to develop their full complexity.

"You're thinking about something deep," Nate observed quietly as Signora Benedetti stepped away to answer a phone call.

"Just about time," Sophie replied. "How long things really take to become what they're meant to be."

They shared a platter of local specialties—pecorino aged in caves, prosciutto sliced paper-thin, and thick slices of bread drizzled with the Benedettis' own olive oil. The combination of flavors triggered a sudden, vivid memory of childhood visits to her grandmother's kitchen, where everything was made from scratch and meals were events that brought families together.

"My grandmother used to make cheese and honey sandwiches for me," Sophie said, surprising herself with the revelation. "Simple white bread, farmer's cheese, and wildflower honey. I thought it was the most sophisticated food in the world."

"How old were you?" Nate asked.

"Maybe seven or eight. After my parents divorced, I spent summers with her in Vermont. She had this tiny garden where she grew herbs and vegetables, and she knew every farmer in the county." Sophie paused, realizing something. "I think that's where my love of farm-to-table food really started—watching her create magic from simple, local ingredients."

"Does she know about your current adventures in investigative food blogging?"

Sophie's smile faded. "She died when I was in college. But I think she would have loved Marco's story. She understood the connection between food and justice, between how we treat the land and how we treat each other."

Nate reached across the small table and covered her hand with his. "She would be proud of you. What you've accomplished here—it's exactly the kind of work that honors that connection."

The simple touch sent warmth up Sophie's arm, and she found herself studying Nate's face in the golden afternoon light. There were lines around his eyes that hadn't been there when she'd left Sonoma, evidence of his own stresses and worries. She realized she'd never asked what it had cost him to drop everything and fly to Italy when she needed help.

"Nate," she said carefully, "I never thanked you properly for coming. For risking your own safety to help people you'd never met."

"You don't need to thank me," he replied, but his hand remained on hers. "Sophie, when I got your messages about murder and mineral deposits, I was terrified. Not just because you were in danger, but because I realized how much you'd come to mean to me."

The admission hung in the air between them, weighted with months of careful friendship and unspoken possibilities. Sophie felt her heart rate increase, but not with the panicked anxiety that had characterized her relationship with Ryan. This felt different—safer, more solid.

"I almost didn't come," Nate continued, his voice quiet but steady. "I kept thinking that you'd made it clear in Sonoma that you needed space to figure things out. That maybe I'd be overstepping if I just showed up in Italy."

"What changed your mind?"

"The thought that you might not make it home safely." His thumb traced a small circle on the back of her hand. "And the realization that I'd regret not telling you how I felt more than I'd regret being told you weren't ready to hear it."

Sophie looked down at their joined hands, processing the weight of his words. Six months ago, she would have panicked at such a declaration, would have immediately started cataloging all the reasons why romantic complications would derail her carefully planned independence.

Now, she found herself considering possibilities instead of obstacles.

"I'm still figuring things out," she said honestly. "and I don't know where I'll be living next month, let alone next year."

"I'm not asking for certainty," Nate replied. "I'm just asking you not to rule out the possibility that we might figure some things out together."

Signora Benedetti returned to refill their wine glasses, tactfully ignoring the intensity of their conversation while somehow managing to convey approval through her warm smile.

"The afternoon light is perfect for walking through the vineyards," she suggested. "The grapes are almost ready for harvest—you should see them while they're still on the vine."

They thanked her and made their way outside, where the slanted sunlight turned the hillside vineyard into something that belonged on postcards. The grape clusters hung heavy and dark, almost ready for the harvest that would transform them into wine like the Brunello they'd just tasted.

"It's beautiful," Sophie said, pulling out her camera to capture the interplay of light and shadow across the rows of vines.

"Everything about this place is beautiful," Nate replied, but when Sophie looked up, he was watching her rather than the landscape.

The moment stretched between them, charged with potential and weighted with the knowledge that tomorrow would bring separation and uncertainty. Sophie lowered her camera and took a step closer to him.

"Nate," she said, and then stopped, unsure how to articulate the complexity of what she was feeling.

"I know," he said softly. "It's complicated. The timing is terrible. You're still processing a major life change, and I live three thousand miles away from wherever you're going next."

"All of that is true," Sophie agreed.

"But?"

"But I also know that I've never felt safer with anyone than I do with you. And I've never met someone who understood my work—my real work—the way you do."

They were standing close enough now that she could see the flecks of gold in his brown eyes, could smell the faint scent of his cologne mixed with the wine they'd shared.

"Sophie," he said, and she could hear the question in his voice.

Instead of answering with words, she rose on her toes and kissed him.

It was gentle at first—tentative, exploratory, nothing like the desperate passion that had characterized her early relationship with Ryan. This felt like a conversation, a careful exchange of possibility and promise. When Nate's arms came around her, she felt herself relax into the embrace rather than tensing with anxiety about what it might mean.

When they finally separated, Sophie rested her forehead against his, both of them breathing a little unsteadily.

"Well," she said after a moment. "That was... clarifying."

Nate laughed, the sound warm and relieved. "Good clarifying or concerning clarifying?"

"Definitely good clarifying." Sophie stepped back slightly, needing space to think clearly. "But Nate, I need you to know—I'm not ready to make any big decisions about the future. I'm still figuring out who I am outside of my marriage, outside of the life I thought I wanted."

"I wouldn't want you to rush that process," he replied seriously. "Sophie, you've been through massive changes in the past six months. The last thing you need is pressure to commit to something new before you're ready."

"So what are you saying?"

"I'm saying that I care about you enough to be patient. To let you set the pace. To be whatever you need me to be —friend, occasional visitor, long-distance whatever-this-is." He gestured between them. "I just don't want us to lose touch again."

Sophie felt something ease in her chest that she hadn't realized was tense. This was what had been missing with Ryan—the patience, the willingness to let her be uncertain without demanding immediate answers.

"I don't want to lose touch either," she said. "But I also don't want you waiting around for me to figure my life out. You deserve someone who knows what they want."

"Right now, I want you to have the time and space to heal completely from your marriage," Nate said. "I want you to explore whatever opportunities come your way. And I want to know that when you're ready—if you're ready—there's something real here worth exploring."

They walked back toward the winery in comfortable silence, the conversation having cleared the air without forcing premature conclusions. Sophie felt lighter some-how, as if acknowledging the possibility of something developing between them had paradoxically reduced the pressure to define it immediately.

"One more thing," Nate said as they reached the car. "Whatever happens between us, I want you to know that watching you work this week—seeing you fight for justice and refuse to be intimidated—has been incredible.

You're not the same person who left Oregon six months ago."

"No," Sophie agreed, thinking about the woman who Ryan's betrayal had so shattered that she'd fled across the country. "I'm not. And I'm finally starting to like who I'm becoming."

As they drove back down the winding road toward Montepulciano, Sophie felt a sense of completion that had nothing to do with romance and everything to do with self-acceptance. She had kissed Nate because she wanted to, not because she felt pressured or desperate for validation. She had been honest about her uncertainty without apologizing for it.

For the first time in her adult life, she was learning to trust her own timing.

Her phone buzzed with a message from Oliver:

> Oliver: Darling, I just saw the CNN interview request. Please tell me you're not about to become one of those serious journalists who forgets to be fabulous. The world needs your particular brand of chaos and cuisine! 🍸

> Sophie: Still fabulous, still chaotic. But maybe with better investigative instincts now. How do you feel about being the best friend of an international correspondent?

> Oliver: As long as you promise to send me exotic snacks from every country you visit, I'm entirely supportive of your new career path. Just remember us little people when you're winning Pulitzers!

As they pulled into the farmhouse drive, Sophie caught sight of Sofia in the kitchen window, preparing what looked like an elaborate dinner. The sight filled her with warmth—the knowledge that she'd found a chosen family in this unlikely place, that leaving tomorrow wouldn't mean losing the connections she'd forged.

Later that evening, as they gathered around Sofia's table, Sophie noticed the unread voicemail still sitting in her phone—Ryan's latest attempt at a conversation, a coffee shop meeting she'd never agreed to. She hovered over the play button, then quietly deleted the message. She didn't need to hear his justifications anymore. She already knew the difference between a man who loved her as a mirror and one who saw her as herself.

"Thank you," she said to Nate as they gathered their things from the car.

"For what?"

"For being patient. For understanding that some things can't be rushed." She paused, then added with a small smile, "And for being an excellent kisser."

Nate's laughter followed her into the house, where the scent of Sofia's cooking and the promise of one last evening in Tuscany waited to welcome them home.

———

*From Sophie's Substack: **Farm-to-Table Adventures***

"Today I learned that the best tastings aren't just about wine or food—they're about savoring moments of possibility. Some flavors develop slowly, requiring patience and the right conditions to reach their full potential. In Tuscany, I'm discovering that the same might be true for matters of the heart."

CHAPTER 17
RYAN'S GOODBYE

THE TRAIN to Florence cut through the Tuscan countryside with rhythmic precision, carrying Sophie away from the olive groves and toward a conversation she'd been avoiding for six months. She'd deleted Ryan's voicemail without listening, but his follow-up text had been impossible to ignore: "I know you're angry, but I'm flying back to the States tomorrow. Can we please talk? I'll wait at Caffè Pitti until you arrive or my flight departs. Your choice."

Nate had offered to come with her, but Sophie had declined. This was something she needed to do alone—not because she owed Ryan anything, but because she owed herself the closure of ending things properly instead of running away again.

The train pulled into Firenze Santa Maria Novella as the morning gave way to late afternoon. Sophie made her way through the familiar chaos of the station—tourists consulting maps, locals hurrying past with practiced efficiency, the constant announcements echoing in Italian and

English. Florence felt different than it had during her brief visit months ago. Then, she'd been a tourist escaping her problems. Now, she was a woman returning to face them.

Caffè Pitti sat on a quiet side street near the Palazzo Pitti, the kind of place that served excellent espresso to locals while remaining largely undiscovered by the tour groups. Sophie spotted Ryan through the window before she entered—he sat at a corner table, checking his phone obsessively, his usually perfect hair slightly messed as if he'd been running his hands through it.

He looked up as she entered, and Sophie was surprised by the relief that flooded his features. She'd expected his usual confident charm, the polished exterior that had attracted her initially and frustrated her endlessly by the end of their marriage.

"Sophie," he said, rising from his chair. "Thank you for coming. I wasn't sure you would."

"I almost didn't," she replied honestly, settling into the chair across from him. The café was nearly empty—the afternoon lull between lunch and evening aperitivo when even the most dedicated coffee drinkers took a break.

Ryan signaled the waitress, who brought Sophie an espresso without being asked. The small gesture reminded her of their early years together, when he'd known her preferences, when attention to detail had felt like love rather than control.

"You look good," he said carefully. "Different. Stronger, maybe."

Sophie sipped her espresso, studying the man she'd been married to for five years. He was still handsome in the classic American way that turned heads in European cities—tall, well-dressed, confident in his occupation of space. But something had changed in his demeanor. The easy assumption that he could charm his way through any situation seemed frayed around the edges.

"Ryan," she said, "why are we here? What is it you need to say that you couldn't wait until we're both back in the States?"

He was quiet for a moment, turning his own cup in small circles on the marble table. "I've been reading about what you've accomplished here—the investigation, the arrests, the international coverage. I'm proud of you, Sophie. And I'm ashamed of myself."

"For which part?"

"All of it." His voice carried a rawness she'd rarely heard before. "For lying about the suppliers in Oregon. For making decisions without consulting you. For treating our partnership like it was my business and your hobby." He paused, meeting her eyes directly. "For making you feel like you had to run away to find out who you really were."

Sophie had imagined this conversation countless times during the dark months after leaving Oregon. In some versions, she'd been angry and accusatory. In others, coolly dismissive. She'd never imagined feeling this strange mixture of sadness and detachment, as if she were watching someone else's marriage dissolve from a safe distance.

"Why now?" she asked. "Why this sudden insight into your behavior?"

Ryan's laugh was bitter. "Because watching you succeed without me made me realize what I'd lost. And because my therapist finally got through to me about what I'd done to you."

"You're in therapy?"

"Started three months ago, after I realized that losing you wasn't just bad luck or poor timing. It was a direct result of my choices." He reached into his jacket and withdrew a folded document. "Sophie, I know this might not matter to you anymore, but I need you to know that I never meant to diminish you. I thought I was protecting our business, but I was really just protecting my ego."

Sophie recognized the papers immediately—divorce documents, already signed in Ryan's careful handwriting. The sight of them should have felt like victory, but instead, she felt a complicated mix of relief and melancholy.

"You signed them," she said quietly.

"I signed them because you deserve better than being married to someone who took five years to learn how to appreciate you." Ryan slid the papers across the table. "I'm not giving up because I don't love you. I'm giving up because I finally understand what love actually requires."

Sophie stared at the documents that would officially end their marriage. She'd expected this moment to feel triumphant, but instead, she found herself mourning the loss of the good years, the dreams they'd shared before ambition and dishonesty had poisoned everything.

"Do you remember our first date?" Ryan asked suddenly.

"The farmers market in Portland," Sophie replied without thinking. "You bought me coffee and a basket of strawberries, and we ended up talking for four hours about sustainable agriculture."

"You were so passionate about the connection between food and community. You made me see ingredients as stories instead of just products." His smile was genuine but sad. "I fell in love with that passion, Sophie. And then I spent five years trying to make it more practical, more profitable, more like what I thought a business should be."

"You fell in love with a version of me that you wanted to improve," Sophie said, the realization settling over her with startling clarity. "You loved my passion as long as you could direct it."

Ryan winced, but nodded. "I told myself I was being supportive. But you're right—I was trying to manage you instead of partnering with you."

They sat in silence for a moment, the weight of acknowledged truth settling between them. Sophie found herself thinking about Nate, about the way he'd encouraged her investigation without trying to control its direction, the way he'd supported her choices even when they put her in danger.

"There's someone else," Ryan said. It wasn't a question.

"There might be," Sophie replied honestly. "But that's not why I can't come back to you."

"I know." Ryan reached across the table as if to take her hand, then stopped himself. "Sophie, will you tell me what it is? What I could have done differently?"

Sophie considered the question, searching for words that would be honest without being cruel. "You could have trusted me. Trusted my judgment, my instincts, my ability to handle difficult information. You could have treated me like an equal partner instead of someone who needed to be protected from the complexities of our own business."

"I thought I was being a good husband," Ryan said quietly.

"You were being a good manager," Sophie replied. "But marriage isn't a business relationship. It requires a different kind of partnership."

The waitress refilled their cups without being asked, moving with the practiced discretion of someone who'd witnessed countless difficult conversations in this quiet corner café. Sophie found herself grateful for the interruption, the chance to process what felt like the most honest conversation she and Ryan had ever had.

"Can I ask you something?" Ryan said eventually.

"Of course."

"Are you happy? I mean, really happy, not just relieved to be away from our problems."

Sophie considered the question, thinking about the past week—the terror and triumph, the friendships forged in crisis, the satisfaction of seeing justice served. "I'm becoming happy," she said finally. "I'm learning to trust my own instincts, to take risks for things that matter. I'm discovering that I'm braver than I thought I was."

"Good," Ryan said, and she could hear that he meant it. "You deserve to be brave. You deserve someone who celebrates that instead of trying to contain it."

They talked for another hour, reminiscing about good times and acknowledging bad ones. It felt like emotional archaeology, carefully excavating the remains of something that had once been vital. By the time they finished, Sophie felt lighter, as if she'd been carrying the weight of unfinished business for months without realizing it.

"I should go," Ryan said finally, checking his watch. "My flight leaves in three hours."

They stood together, and for a moment, Sophie saw a flash of the young man she'd fallen in love with—idealistic, passionate about making a difference in the world, before success had complicated his motivations.

"Ryan," she said as they prepared to part ways. "I hope

you find what you're looking for. I hope you find someone who brings out the best in you instead of making you feel like you need to be someone else."

"I hope I become someone worthy of that," he replied.

They embraced briefly—a goodbye that carried finality rather than longing. When they separated, Sophie felt the strange peace that comes with ending something properly instead of letting it fade away through neglect and resentment.

She walked alone through the streets of Florence as evening approached, the golden light that made the city famous beginning to paint the ancient buildings in warm tones. The Arno River reflected the sky like a mirror, and Sophie found herself following its banks without any particular destination in mind.

Her phone buzzed with a message from Nate:

> Nate: How did it go? Are you okay?

She typed back:

> Sophie: It went well. Sad, but clean. I'm walking along the river, thinking about everything.

> Nate: Take all the time you need. I'll be here when you're ready.

Sophie smiled at his response, appreciating the lack of pressure or demand for immediate details. This was what she'd been missing—someone who understood that processing difficult emotions required space and patience.

As the sun set over Florence, painting the sky in shades of gold and rose, Sophie sent another message:

> Sophie: I'm coming home.

> Nate: To Tuscany?

> Sophie: To wherever we go next.

The response came quickly:

> Nate: I can live with that level of uncertainty. 😊

There was a pause as three dots appeared.

> Nate: Though part of me wonders if I'm out of my depth here. I told myself back in Sonoma not to get pulled into your mysteries. But then again… here I am.

Sophie smiled, tucked her phone away and continued walking along the river, feeling the last weight of her marriage finally lifting from her shoulders. The divorce was already final, but tonight it felt truly finished—not just on paper, but in her heart.

She thought about Marco's journal, about his documentation of a life fully lived in service of things that mattered. She thought about Sofia's courage in standing up for her family's legacy. She thought about Elena's fierce protection of her grandson, and Nate's willingness to cross an ocean because someone he cared about needed help.

These were the models she wanted to follow—people who chose love and justice and truth over comfort and convenience. People who understood that the best things in life required courage to pursue and commitment to maintain.

Her phone rang, Oliver's name appearing on the screen.

"Darling!" his familiar voice filled her with warmth. "Please tell me you haven't decided to reconcile with the lying restaurateur and move back to Oregon."

"No chance," Sophie replied, smiling despite the emotional exhaustion of the day. "The divorce papers are signed, filed, and finished."

"Thank God. I was prepared to stage an intervention involving large quantities of wine and possibly a kidnapping." Oliver's tone grew more serious. "How are you feeling? Really?"

"Sad," Sophie said honestly. "But also free. It's like I've been carrying something heavy for so long that I forgot what it felt like to stand up straight."

"And the delicious Italian restaurant owner who flew across the world to rescue you?"

"He's not Italian, he's from California. And he didn't rescue me—he supported me while I rescued myself."

"Even better," Oliver replied with satisfaction. "Sophie, I'm proud of you. For the investigation, for standing up to criminals, for ending your marriage with grace instead of spite. You've become quite formidable."

"I'm learning," Sophie said, watching the lights begin to twinkle in the buildings along the river. "I'm finally learning to trust myself."

After they hung up, Sophie made her way to the train station, ready to return to Tuscany for her final night at the farmhouse. Tomorrow, Nate would fly back to California to settle his affairs, while she would remain in Italy a little longer, following the threads of her new life. But they had already agreed: this wasn't goodbye. Their journeys were converging now, and soon, they would decide together where "home" truly was.

But tonight, she would sleep peacefully for the first time in months, knowing that she had faced her past with honesty and was walking into her future with clear eyes and an open heart.

The train carried her back through the darkening countryside, past olive groves and vineyards that had witnessed centuries of human drama. Some stories ended with tragedy, others with triumph. Sophie's story—the one that had begun with betrayal and heartbreak in Oregon—was ending with wisdom and the promise of new beginnings.

As Tuscany welcomed her home, Sophie Brooks was finally, completely free.

---

*FROM SOPHIE'S SUBSTACK: **Farm-to-Table Adventures***

"Today I learned that the most important ingredient in any recipe for happiness is the courage to start fresh when something isn't working. Some flavors can't be saved, no matter how much you want them to work. But when you're brave enough to clear the palate, you create space for something better to develop."

CHAPTER 18
THE CELEBRATION PRESS

SOPHIE RETURNED from Florence to find the De Luca farmhouse transformed. What had been a place of mourning and crisis just days before now hummed with the quiet energy of celebration. Garlands of olive branches draped the doorways, and the kitchen table groaned under platters of food that spoke to Tuscan abundance—wheels of aged pecorino, baskets of late-season figs, bottles of wine that caught the lamplight like liquid garnets.

"You're back," Sofia said, emerging from the kitchen with flour dusting her apron and relief written across her features. "How did it go?"

"It went well," Sophie replied, setting down her bag and accepting Sofia's embrace. "Sad, but necessary. It's finished now."

Nate appeared in the doorway, and the smile that spread across his face when he saw her made Sophie's heart flutter with possibility. They didn't speak—just shared a look that communicated everything about closure and new beginnings and the courage to move forward.

"Perfect timing," Antonio announced, appearing with a bottle of the family's reserve Chianti. "We were just about to begin the pressing ceremony."

Sophie looked around in confusion. "Pressing ceremony?"

"For *Nonno*," Sofia explained, her voice warm with tradition and love. "Every year after the harvest festival, our family conducts a private pressing of the first olives. It's symbolic—taking the fruit that represents our heritage and transforming it into the oil that will sustain us through the year."

"This year feels especially important," Antonio added. "After everything that's happened, we want to honor his memory properly."

Elena appeared from the pantry carrying a basket of olives that gleamed like dark jewels. "These are from the disputed grove," she announced with satisfaction. "The ones that Vincenzo wanted so badly. It seems fitting that they should be the first pressed in Marco's honor."

Little Marco followed behind his grandmother, his earlier trauma replaced by the resilient bounce of childhood. When he saw Sophie, his face lit up with recognition and shy pleasure.

"Signora Sophie! Did you stop the bad guys? Like superheroes do?"

Sophie knelt to his level, her heart swelling at the light in his eyes. "It wasn't just me, Marco. Your family stood strong, your nonna, your papa, everyone. Together we protected what matters most."

The boy nodded solemnly, then brightened. "Will you help with the pressing? *Nonna* Elena says you have magic hands for cooking."

Sophie felt tears prick her eyes at the invitation to participate in something so deeply rooted in family tradition. "I would be honored."

They made their way to the barn where Marco's antique olive press waited—a massive wooden contraption that had served the family for over a century. Unlike the modern equipment used for commercial production, this press required patience and many hands working in harmony.

The process was ceremonial, almost meditative. Sofia and Elena sorted the olives by hand, removing any damaged fruit and leaves with the careful attention of women who understood that quality oil began with perfect ingredients. Antonio operated the grinding stones, crushing the olives into a thick paste that released the green, peppery aroma that defined Tuscan oil.

Nate worked the press itself, his photographer's hands surprisingly adept at the precise adjustments needed to maintain steady pressure. Sophie found herself spreading the olive paste onto woven mats, layering them carefully in the ancient pattern Sofia demonstrated.

"*Nonno* always said that making oil was like making memories," Sofia explained as they worked. "Slow, careful, requiring the right people at the right time."

As the first drops of golden-green oil began to flow from the press, Elena whispered something in Italian that sounded like a prayer. Little Marco watched with wide eyes, clearly understanding that he was witnessing something sacred.

"What did she say?" Sophie asked Sofia quietly.

"She thanked Marco's spirit for protecting the olives

and asked him to bless this year's oil with the love he put into the land."

The pressing continued for two hours, a slow revelation of liquid gold that filled ceramic urns with the essence of the disputed grove. When they finished, Sofia ceremoniously filled a small glass bottle with the first pressing—oil so fresh it was cloudy with suspended particles, so pure it tasted like concentrated sunlight.

"For you," she said, pressing the bottle into Sophie's hands. "To remember this place, these people, this time when you helped save our family's soul."

Sophie accepted the gift with trembling hands, understanding that she was receiving more than olive oil. This was a token of acceptance, a symbol of belonging that transcended nationality or blood relation.

"Thank you," she whispered. "I'll treasure it."

As if the pressing ceremony had been a signal, neighbors began arriving for an impromptu celebration dinner. Paolo Bianchi appeared with his wife, carrying bottles of his own wine and wearing an expression of peace Sophie hadn't seen before. The local priest arrived with bread still warm from the convent ovens. Even some of the vendors from the market appeared, drawn by the community's need to gather and celebrate survival.

The dinner that followed was a masterclass in Tuscan hospitality. *Pappa al pomodoro*—thick tomato and bread soup enriched with the newly pressed oil—filled earthenware bowls with comfort that spoke to childhood memories. *Fettunta* appeared next—thick slices of grilled bread rubbed with garlic and anointed with the green oil, topped with coarse salt that made the flavors sing.

"This is what Vincenzo never understood," Paolo said

quietly to Sophie as they shared a plate of the bread. "He saw the land as a resource to be extracted. We see it as a partner in creation."

As the evening progressed and wine loosened tongues, stories began to flow. Tales of Marco's generosity, his stubborn dedication to traditional methods, his quiet support of families struggling to maintain their farms.

"He once lent us equipment for three months when our press broke down," one farmer shared. "Refused any payment, said helping neighbors was what the equipment was for."

Elena stood as the evening grew late, raising her glass of wine with ceremony. "To Marco De Luca," she declared, her voice carrying across the gathering. "Who taught us that some things are worth more than money. Who died protecting not just his land, but our way of life."

"To Marco!" the crowd chorused, and Sophie felt the power of community grief transformed into celebration.

Nate found Sophie later on the farmhouse porch, where she sat with her laptop writing her final blog post from Tuscany. The night air carried the scent of cooling earth and the distant sound of laughter from the barn where some guests still lingered.

"Writing the story?" he asked, settling beside her on the wooden bench.

"Trying to," Sophie replied. "How do you capture something like tonight? The pressing ceremony, the dinner, the way an entire community came together to honor one man's memory?"

"The same way you captured everything else— honestly, from the heart."

Sophie saved her draft and closed the laptop, suddenly

aware that tomorrow Nate would fly back to California and she would be left to figure out her next steps alone. The thought created an unexpected hollow in her chest.

"Nate," she began, then stopped, unsure how to voice her uncertainty about saying goodbye.

He was quiet for a moment, his gaze fixed on the olive groves that stretched into darkness. "Sophie, there's something I wanted to talk to you about. Something that might change how we think about tomorrow."

Her pulse quickened. "What do you mean?"

"I've been offered a consulting job. Something that would let me travel, work with food producers in different countries." He paused, watching her face carefully. "The investigative journalism contacts I mentioned? They're launching a documentary series about sustainable food systems around the world."

Sophie felt her heart sink. More travel, more time apart, just when she was beginning to understand what they might mean to each other.

"That sounds amazing," she said, meaning it despite her disappointment. "Where would it take you?"

"Everywhere, eventually. But they want to start with a segment on South African wine and food markets. Cape Town specifically." Nate's smile was carefully neutral. "The producer mentioned they'd love to work with a food writer who has experience with investigative journalism. Someone who understands both cuisine and the social issues surrounding food production."

Sophie stared at him, her mind racing to process the implications. "Are you saying what I think you're saying?"

"I'm saying that if you were interested in exploring Cape Town's food scene for a few months, you wouldn't have to do it alone. And if you decided that documentary work appealed to you more than solo blog writing, there might be opportunities to develop in that direction."

Sophie felt excitement building in her chest, but underneath it was something more complex. This was an incredible opportunity, but she needed to be sure she was choosing it for the right reasons. The memory of Ryan's controlling guidance flickered through her mind—how he'd shaped her career choices around his vision rather than her own instincts.

"It sounds incredible," she said slowly. "But Nate, I need to know that this is a real partnership. That you're not trying to rescue me or manage my career path."

His expression grew serious. "Sophie, I've watched you solve a murder, expose an international conspiracy, and stand up to armed criminals. You don't need rescuing. What I'm offering is collaboration with someone whose instincts I trust completely."

"I spent five years letting someone else make my professional decisions," Sophie said. "I need to be sure I'm choosing this because it's what I want, not because it's easier than figuring out my own path."

"Then take time to decide," Nate replied. "The offer stands whether you say yes tomorrow or in six months. Your story, your timeline, your choice."

Sophie looked at him—really looked—and saw not the controlling partner she'd escaped in Oregon, but someone offering genuine partnership. The difference was profound.

"I would love that," she said simply. "The work, the travel, the chance to explore what we might be together without pressure or deadlines."

"No pressure," Nate agreed. "Just possibility."

As if summoned by their conversation, Sophie's phone buzzed with a message from Oliver:

> Oliver: Darling, please tell me you're not about to disappear into domestic bliss with the California restaurateur. The world needs more of your magnificent meddling! Also, a little bird told me Netflix is interested in your story? 🖥️

Sophie showed the message to Nate, who laughed at Oliver's characteristic blend of concern and excitement.

"He's not wrong about the Netflix interest," Nate said. "One of my documentary contacts mentioned that streaming services are very interested in true crime stories with international elements."

"The Sophie Brooks story, coming to Netflix," Sophie mused. "That feels surreal."

Sophie typed back to Oliver:

> Sophie: I'm still me, just maybe... a little braver. I'll keep meddling. Just with better lighting and camera angles. And yes, apparently Netflix thinks my chaos makes good television.

Oliver's response was immediate:

> Oliver: Magnificent! Just don't forget us mere mortals when your Substack gets optioned for a Netflix series. I expect a cameo as the dashing best friend who saves you with cocktails and sarcasm.

Sophie turned back to her laptop and began typing her final Tuscan blog post:

From Sophie's Substack: Farm-to-Table Adventures

"Tonight I participated in my first olive pressing ceremony, joining hands with people who have become family to transform fruit into liquid gold. I've learned that the best harvests require patience, community, and the courage to defend what matters most.

Marco De Luca died protecting more than olive trees. He died preserving the idea that some things cannot be bought, sold, or corrupted—that tradition and love and commitment to the land create value that transcends any market price.

Tomorrow I leave Tuscany, but I carry with me the taste of oil pressed by grateful hands, the memory of justice served with community support, and the knowledge that the most important stories are the ones that bring people together rather than tear them apart.

Next month, I'll be writing from Cape Town, South Africa, where new flavors and new adventures await. But first, one final taste of Tuscan perfection—fresh bread, golden oil, coarse salt, and the satisfaction of work well done."

Sophie hit publish and closed her laptop, feeling the completion that came with ending one chapter and beginning another. Around her, the night settled over the olive groves with the peace of autumn, of harvest completed, of secrets finally told.

Tomorrow would bring farewells and new journeys. But tonight, in a farmhouse kitchen filled with the scent of fresh oil and the warmth of chosen family, Sophie Brooks was poised between gratitude and possibility, ready to shape whatever came next—like olives to oil—into something enduring.

From Elena's kitchen notebook, shared with Sophie:

Marco's Olive Oil Cake
This recipe belonged to Marco's mother, and her mother before that. The oil must be fruity, not bitter—choose carefully, as the olives will speak through every bite.

3 large eggs
200g sugar
200ml De Luca extra virgin olive oil
200ml whole milk
250g flour
2 tsp baking powder
Zest of 1 lemon
Handful of fresh rosemary, chopped fine
Powdered sugar for dusting

Beat eggs and sugar until pale. Add oil in a thin stream, then milk. Fold in flour, baking powder, lemon zest, and rosemary. Bake in a lined pan at 180°C for 45 minutes. Dust with sugar while warm.
Serve with morning coffee and the memory of those who taught you that the simplest ingredients, treated with respect, create the most lasting joy.

CHAPTER 19
ONE LAST BITE

THE MORNING MARKET in Siena sprawled across the Piazza del Campo like a Renaissance painting come to life. Sophie and Nate wandered between stalls laden with the last treasures of autumn—glossy chestnuts still warm from roasting, wheels of aged pecorino that perfumed the air with their sharp earthiness, and bottles of new wine so young they still carried the ghost of fermentation.

"I can't believe you're leaving in six hours," Sophie said, pausing to photograph a vendor arranging porcini mushrooms in perfect spirals. The fungi looked like carved wood, their caps gleaming with the kind of natural beauty that made her understand why people fought to preserve traditional food ways.

"We'll figure out how to close the distance soon," Nate said, his tone warm rather than reproachful.

They'd spent the morning saying goodbye to the De Luca family, a process that had involved tears, promises to stay in touch, and Elena pressing enough preserved foods into Sophie's luggage to sustain her through a small siege.

Little Marco had given her another wooden carving—this one a tiny olive tree that fit in her palm like a talisman.

Now they had these few hours before Nate's flight, time to wander through a market that celebrated everything they'd learned to value in Tuscany—patience, tradition, the connection between land and table.

"*Porchetta!*" called a vendor from beneath a striped awning, his voice carrying the musical authority of someone who knew his product was irresistible. "*Fresca, calda, perfetta!*"

Sophie felt her mouth water at the sight of the roasted pork, its skin crackling and dark, carved into thick slices that revealed meat so tender it fell apart at the knife's touch. The vendor assembled their sandwiches with theatrical flair—crusty bread split and filled with the succulent pork, a scatter of fresh herbs, and a drizzle of oil that caught the morning light.

They found a small table at a café overlooking the campo, sharing the sandwich while pigeons strutted hopefully around their feet. The porchetta was everything good Italian food should be—simple, honest, perfect in its execution.

"This is what I'll miss most," Sophie said, taking another bite and closing her eyes to savor the interplay of textures and flavors. "Not just the food, but the way people here treat food as if it matters."

"It does matter," Nate replied. "And you're going to keep telling those stories, whether it's in Cape Town or wherever you end up next."

Sophie had been thinking about next steps since their conversation on the farmhouse porch. The documentary opportunity was compelling, but she'd also received an email that morning from a South African chef named Thandi Mbeki, whose message had been brief but intriguing: *I've been following your work in Italy. Cape Town has stories that need telling, if you're interested in markets that might challenge everything you think you know about food and justice.*

"Actually," Sophie said, wiping her fingers on the paper napkin, "I might have just been offered a food writing opportunity. In Cape Town."

Nate's fork paused halfway to his mouth. "Really? Tell me more."

Sophie pulled out her phone and showed him Thandi's message, watching his face brighten as he read. "She runs a restaurant that sources everything from township markets and small-scale farmers. Apparently she's been documenting some concerning practices in the commercial food distribution system."

"Sounds like you've found your next investigation," Nate said with a grin. "Any chance you'd want company there sometime?"

Sophie felt her heart do that familiar flutter, but now it came with confidence rather than anxiety. "You bring the camera," she said, meeting his eyes directly. "I'll bring the curiosity."

They lingered over their coffee, neither wanting to acknowledge the approaching deadline of Nate's departure. The market around them began to shift into afternoon rhythms—vendors consolidating their displays, shoppers moving with the purposeful energy of people preparing evening meals.

"One more thing," the chestnut vendor called as they passed her stall. She was perhaps seventy, her hands stained dark from handling the roasted nuts, her smile carrying the warmth of someone who'd spent decades watching couples share her treats. "*Castagnaccio* for the beautiful lovers. To sweeten your goodbye."

She pressed a slice of chestnut cake into Sophie's hands —dense, dark, studded with pine nuts and raisins, carrying the concentrated sweetness of autumn concentrated into edible form. Sophie broke off a piece for Nate, and they ate standing beside the stall, the cake's rustic sweetness providing a perfect counterpoint to the morning's savory indulgences.

"*Grazie*," Sophie said to the vendor, who waved away her attempt to pay.

"*Amore* is its own payment," the woman replied with a knowing smile.

As they walked back through the medieval streets toward where they'd parked, Nate stopped suddenly at a small shop tucked between a wine bar and a bakery. The window display showed jars of what looked like mud but carried a hand-lettered sign: *Tartufi Freschi - Fresh Truffles*.

"One last bite," he said, pulling her inside.

The shop was tiny, just large enough for the proprietor —a serious man in his sixties who handled his products with the reverence of a museum curator. He showed them slices of truffle that looked unremarkable but smelled like the essence of earth and autumn concentrated into something almost mystical.

They sampled the truffles on simple crackers with a touch of good butter, the flavor exploding across Sophie's palate with an intensity that made her understand why people paid fortunes for these strange fungi. It tasted like the forest floor after rain, like secrets buried in dark soil, like the mystery of how something so humble could contain such complexity.

"That," Sophie said after swallowing, "is going to haunt my dreams."

"Good haunting or bad haunting?" Nate asked.

"The best kind. The kind that makes you want to keep exploring, keep tasting, keep discovering what else is out there."

The drive to the airport carried an unexpected lightness. They talked about practical things—his documentary work, her plans to research Cape Town's food scene, the logistics of staying in touch across time zones. But underneath the ordinary conversation ran something steadier: the understanding that this was a beginning rather than an ending.

"Sophie," Nate said as they pulled into the departure area, "what you've accomplished these past few weeks isn't just about solving Marco's murder. You've learned to trust yourself completely. That's going to serve you well wherever you go next."

Sophie felt her throat tighten. "Thank you. For everything."

"See you soon," he said, leaning over to kiss her with the gentleness of someone who understood that the best things couldn't be rushed.

As she drove back through the countryside, Sophie caught sight of the Tuscan hills in her rearview mirror— the same rolling landscape she'd first glimpsed from a taxi window three weeks ago. Then, she'd been running from her problems. Now, she was driving toward her future, carrying the lessons of this place like seeds ready to be planted in new soil.

Her phone buzzed with a message from Oliver:

> Oliver: Darling, please tell me you're not standing in an airport crying over a man. You're far too fabulous for that particular cliché.

> Sophie: Not crying. Planning. Turns out there's a difference between saying goodbye and saying "until next time."

> Oliver: Much better. Now tell me about this South African adventure I've been hearing whispers about.

Sophie smiled, tucking her phone away, leaving Oliver in suspense for a little while longer as the farmhouse came into view. Tomorrow she would begin the journey toward whatever came next. But tonight, she would write the last blog post of her Tuscan adventure, sharing the story of a market morning that had somehow contained the perfect farewell.

Some flavors, she'd discovered, were worth crossing oceans to experience again.

---

*FROM SOPHIE'S SUBSTACK: **Farm-to-Table Adventures***
"This morning I said goodbye to someone important while sharing porchetta, chestnut cake, and truffles that tasted like edible poetry. I'm learning that the best farewells aren't about ending but about carrying the best parts of an experience forward into whatever comes next. Some flavors linger on the palate long after the meal is finished—and sometimes, that's exactly as it should be."

EPILOGUE - "PRESSED, BUT NOT BROKEN"

From Sophie's Substack: Farm-to-Table Adventures

    I'm writing this final post from the De Luca farmhouse kitchen, where morning light streams through windows that have watched over olive groves for more than two centuries. The scent of fresh coffee mingles with the lingering perfume of yesterday's bread, and in the next room I can hear Sofia humming quietly as she folds laundry, flour still dusting her cheek from this morning's baking. In a few hours, I'll pack my bags and begin the journey toward my next adventure. But first, I want to share what Tuscany has taught me about patience, truth, and the kind of courage that develops slowly—like good oil from fruit that's waited generations to reveal its secrets.

    When I arrived here three weeks ago, I thought I was documenting traditional olive oil production. Instead, I discovered that some stories require you to dig deeper than the surface, to follow instincts that whisper rather than shout, and to understand that the most important harvests often come from the most unlikely soil.

    Marco De Luca's murder wasn't solved through brilliant

deduction or lucky breaks. It was solved through the patient accumulation of details—a journal entry here, a financial record there, conversations that revealed more in what wasn't said than in what was. Marco himself taught me this, through his careful documentation of everything from weather patterns to family grudges. He understood that truth emerges slowly, like oil pressed from olives that have spent months ripening in Mediterranean sunshine.

Before his death, Marco shared with me a recipe that his grandmother had passed down through five generations of De Luca women. It's simple—preserved lemons and olives transformed into something that captures the essence of this place in every bite. But like everything truly valuable, it can't be rushed.

Marco's Grandmother's Olive and Preserved Lemon Tapenade

This recipe requires patience twice—first to preserve the lemons, then to let the flavors marry. Like a good marriage or a good friendship, it gets better with time.

For the preserved lemons (begin 1 month ahead):
10 organic lemons, scrubbed clean
Coarse sea salt
Bay leaves

Quarter the lemons from the top to within 1/2 inch of the bottom. Stuff with salt and pack in a sterilized jar with bay leaves. Press down firmly—they must be covered by their own juice. Wait 30 days, turning the jar occasionally.

Note: Once preserved, these lemons transform any dish—chop them into grain salads, blend into salad dressings, or stuff under chicken skin before roasting. The brine makes an excellent addition to cocktails or marinades.

For the tapenade:

1 cup Kalamata olives, pitted
2 preserved lemons, pulp removed, rinds chopped fine
2 cloves garlic
2 tablespoons capers
1/4 cup best olive oil you can find
Fresh thyme leaves
Crack of black pepper

Pulse everything in a food processor until roughly chopped—you want texture, not paste. Taste and adjust. Serve on grilled bread with a glass of something that makes you feel grateful.

The lemons must cure in their own tears before they can bring sweetness to others. Sometimes people are the same.

This recipe embodies everything I've learned in Tuscany. The preserved lemons represent the necessity of time—some transformations can't be hurried, no matter how impatient we become. The olives remind us that even bitter fruit can become something beautiful when handled with care. And the combination of the two creates something entirely new while honoring the individual character of each ingredient.

Six months ago, I was like a fresh lemon—sharp, unprocessed, full of potential but not yet ready to contribute to something larger than myself. My marriage had ended, my confidence was shattered, and I was running from pain rather than processing it into wisdom.

Tuscany became my salt and time—the preservation process that transformed bitterness into something useful. Marco's murder investigation forced me to follow hunches I'd previously ignored. Confronting Vincenzo's conspiracy taught me that justice requires courage, not just good intentions. And learning to accept help from people like Sofia, Elena, and Nate showed me the difference between dependence and healthy partnership.

Some truths take generations to mature. Some flavors, too. Marco's family had been guardian of secrets for eighty years, protecting not just their land but the values it represented. Vincenzo's defeat wasn't just the arrest of a criminal—it was the preservation of a way of life that values patience over profit, community over competition, tradition over trendy shortcuts.

Tomorrow I begin the next chapter of this journey. I'll be traveling to Cape Town, South Africa, where a chef named Thandi Mbeki has promised to show me markets that "challenge everything you think you know about food and justice." Given what I've learned about my own capacity for surprise, I suspect she's right.

But tonight, I'll sit on the farmhouse porch with a glass of wine pressed from grapes that grew in soil enriched by centuries of olive leaves. I'll listen to Sofia and Antonio planning tomorrow's harvest work, their voices carrying the same rhythms of seasonal planning that Marco's voice once carried. Elena will stop by with little Marco, who will show me his latest wooden carving and ask when I'm coming back to visit. I'll taste the tapenade that connects me to five generations of women who understood that the best recipes are passed down not just through ingredients and instructions, but through the stories that give them meaning.

The olive trees outside my window have survived wars, plagues, economic collapse, and the changing whims of human ambition. They're still here, still producing fruit, still teaching patience to anyone willing to learn. Tomorrow I'll carry their lessons with me to a new continent, a new investigation, and new opportunities to press truth from whatever complications await.

Next month, I'll be reporting from the Southern Hemisphere —where I've been promised a market full of spice, story, and maybe a little mischief. Until then, arrivederci from Tuscany, where I learned that some harvests are worth waiting for, some secrets are worth protecting, and some people are worth crossing oceans to see again.

With gratitude and a suitcase full of olive oil,

Sophie Brooks

P.S. — For those asking about the Netflix documentary rumors: yes, they're true. No, I haven't decided yet. Some stories are too important to risk getting wrong, even for Hollywood money. But if you see a slightly terrified food blogger standing next to a very patient cameraman in some exotic location, that might be me learning to trust the process all over again.

Sophie closed her laptop and set it aside, feeling the satisfying completion that came with ending one story while opening the door to the next. Through the kitchen window, she could see Elena walking up the path with little Marco, their evening visit as reliable as clockwork.

Sofia appeared in the doorway, wiping her hands on a dish towel, her face bright with the kind of contentment that came from work well done and family safely gathered.

Outside, the olive groves settled into evening quiet, and somewhere in the distance, she could hear Nate's plane crossing the night sky toward California.

But this wasn't an ending. It was a pressing—taking everything she'd learned and experienced, applying gentle but persistent pressure, and seeing what golden truth might emerge.

Some harvests, she'd discovered, were just the beginning.

The End

Did you enjoy *Olives and Obsessions*?
Please consider rating or reviewing it on Goodreads, Bookbub or your favorite retailer.

Read *Markets & Mysteries*, the next book in the **Sophie Brooks Mysteries.**

Have you read the FREE prequel?
Download *Feasts and Farewells*, Sophie's short origin story.

ABOUT THE AUTHOR

Daisy Landish is a clean romance and cozy mystery author whose clean and sweet novellas have tugged at readers' heartstrings around the world. When she's not writing love stories, Daisy spends her time reading, hiking at dawn, and riding into the sunset on her horse, Rosebud.

Join Daisy's Newsletter for updates and giveaways!
www.daisylandishromance.com

facebook.com/daisylandishromance
x.com/daisy_landish
instagram.com/daisylandishbooks
amazon.com/author/daisylandish
bookbub.com/authors/daisy-landish
goodreads.com/Daisy_Landish

ALSO BY DAISY LANDISH

Clean Regency Romance

Christmas with the Earl

The Lady Series - The Allington Collection

The Lady Series - The Gillingham Collection

The Lady Series - The Blackmore Collection

The Lady Series - The Norrington Collection

Clean Contemporary Romance

Timeline Retreats

Maplewood Grove Series

Love on Spruce Island

Second Chance

Cherry Tree Island

The Wedding Trio

Extra Credit

Counting on the Cowboy

Focusing on the Cowboy

Mistletoe Magic

Grounded at Christmas

Cozy Mysteries

Lady Ashcoombe Mysteries

Sophie Brooks Mysteries

Jane and Kennedy Daniels Mysteries

Pine Grove Mysteries

Annie Archer Paranormal Mysteries

Wilma Wade Holiday Mysteries

Mike and Maddie Mysteries

Mystic Moonhaven Mysteries

Cozy Mystery Samplers

Sweater Weather: Cozy Mysteries for Fall

Summer Vibes: Cozy Mysteries for Summer

Let it Snow: Cozy Mysteries for Winter

Spring Break: Cozy Mysteries for Spring